MISSION 9

MANCHURIAN SECTOR

mars DIARIES

MISSION 9

MANCHURIAN SECTOR

SIGMUND BROUWER

TYNDALE KIDS

TYNDALE HOUSE PUBLISHERS, INC.
WHEATON, ILLINOIS

THIS SERIES IS DEDICATED
IN MEMORY OF MARTYN GODFREY.

Martyn, you wrote books that reached all of us kids at heart. You wrote them because you really cared. We all miss you.

CHAPTER 1

Radiation blast!

Behind me, three doors—each three feet thick and made of steel-encased concrete—were already open to the outer world. Ahead was the final door protecting the inner core of the nuclear reactor at the power plant. It was the final barrier between me and the intense heat and radiation about to blast me when a computer signal triggered it to open like the ones behind me.

Had my body been there in my wheelchair, the heat would have made puddles of my skin and flesh, reducing me to bones and skull. Just as deadly were the radiation waves coming from the reactor's uranium core, only a half hour away from a final and catastrophic meltdown.

Fortunately I approached not in my wheelchair, but through a robot body that had rolled under my control through the first three doorways toward that last door. In theory, my task was simple. Pull the rod of uranium from the sheath that fueled the reactor, shutting it down. But I had to do it fast—all before the entire reactor exploded in a mushroom cloud with five times the power of any nuclear bomb.

And all because of bad hamburgers.

Ten hours earlier, a bizarre chain of events had begun the meltdown. First, one of the power plant transformers had been struck by lightning, triggering three key massive surge protectors. This in itself would have done no serious damage. After all, engineers had installed the surge protectors for something exactly like this. What they hadn't planned on was a second lightning bolt hitting the same transformer within the next 10 seconds. Millions of volts had overwhelmed the power plant's internal systems, crashing half the computers and scrambling the other half.

Even so, the problem should have ended there. At any given time, three technicians were on shift to monitor the system. In an emergency such as this one, only two of the technicians are needed to hit twin fail-safe controls on each side of the massive monitoring panel, and a computer would begin shutting down the nuclear reactor.

Shutting down the nuclear reactor wasn't something you wanted to do every day, though. The city of Los Angeles, California, would be shut down because they'd have lost the electrical power supplied by this nuclear plant. And it would take 10 days to complete the shutdown and then get the nuclear core up and running again.

But compared to the alternative, 10 days of blackout was a cheap price to pay. Because if the nuclear core exploded, its shock waves would kill every person within 30 miles. And with the wind blowing as it was, deadly radioactive dust would cover everyone else for another 20 miles beyond to the west.

Which meant all of Los Angeles. With the freeways jammed to a standstill by people trying to flee in panic.

On any other day, the one-in-ten-million chance of a second lightning bolt would have led to an immediate and inconvenient shutdown.

Except for those uncooked hamburgers.

All three night-shift technicians had shared some take-out burgers as they carpooled to work that evening. And all three had gotten violently sick halfway through their shift. With one technician in the bathroom, the other two had stayed, doubled over in agony in front of the controls. That's why they had missed the first warning lights on the control board. Backup sirens had alerted them 30 seconds later. Sick or not, they knew what needed to be done: count down so that each could hit his own shutdown button. Both buttons had to be pressed at exactly the same time to begin the shutdown.

But the retching and dizziness caused by the bad hamburgers had proved to be too much strain for the older of the two remaining technicians. He had fainted and fallen backward as he reached for the shutdown control.

How did I know this? All of it was well documented on the video loop that monitored the control room. With one technician in the bathroom and one unconscious on the control-room floor, the sole technician remaining at the control board was helpless. He could only reach one shutdown control at a time. When the technician returned from the bathroom two minutes later, the nuclear core was out of control.

That's why I'd been sent. I'm Tyce Sanders. Fourteen years old and very new to Earth. I was supposed to be on an urgent secret mission to the Moon: locating a missing pod of kids like me, who could control robots through their own brain waves. Instead, because of this Earth emergency, high-ranking Combat Force military officials had flown me early this morning, 04.02.2040, by supersonic jet from

New York City, where I was supposed to meet with the military higher-ups, to an L.A. military base, with my robot beside me.

As if this wasn't enough stress, just a day earlier, my friend Ashley and I had nearly died. We and our robots helped stop a terrorist plot that would have killed all the Supreme Governors of the World United Federation—what used to be called the *United Nations* when my dad was a kid. Ashley was in the desert mountains of Arizona, helping with all the other robot-control kids who had just been rescued.

And I'd been sent here to California. With the thunderstorm that had begun the blowout long gone, the weather had been perfect for flying. As the jet circled the Los Angeles basin on its approach to the Combat Force base, the military division of the World United Federation, I had a clear view of the almost endless city sprawl and the autopilot vehicles that plugged the highways.

The city was in a valley, guarded by the jagged edges of the green-brown mountains against blue sky. I took in the view with awe since the planet I'd lived on all my life— Mars—looked so different. There the mountains are red, and during the day the sun is blue against a butterscotch-colored sky.

During the approach to the runway—with that view filling the window—thoughts of God and his amazing universe had naturally popped into my head. A little over nine months ago I hadn't even been interested in him. It had taken a crisis—the Mars Dome almost running out of oxygen—to make me even believe there might be a God. And then some more months to realize that he really loved *me, personally*—not just humans in general. My friend Ashley had been a big part of that discovery. That was only one of the many reasons I was glad the director of the Mars Project, Rawling McTigre, had sent Ashley, my dad, and me to Earth together on a mission.

Today was only the beginning of my eighth day on Earth, and already so much had happened. Now I was faced with a nuclear meltdown that had begun 10 hours earlier.

Nuclear plant officials had spoken to me by videophone almost the entire flight, explaining the situation and trying to prepare me for my task. Time was running short, so they couldn't afford to give me instructions on my arrival.

Once the jet touched ground in L.A., it had taken another two hours for the nuclear experts to coach me through the training session. Or, more precisely, for me to run the robot through its training session. Again and again and again. I would only have one chance. If I made the slightest mistake, I might actually trigger an earlier meltdown.

Which would kill me just as surely as everyone else in the meltdown zone. Because I was only a mile away from the nuclear plant, controlling the robot by remote from my wheelchair.

Now the fourth and final door began to open, and I focused all my attention on the task ahead.

I'd already shut down the robot's heat sensors. Although the titanium skin of my robot was far more durable than my own skin, I didn't want my brain to panic, telling me my body was in a furnace.

A vertical bar of intense white heat widened as the door opened more.

I directed my robot to reach up with its right arm and flip down a protective shield of black glass to reduce the glare. Otherwise, with the light rays reaching my brain through the

5

robot's video lenses, it would be like staring into the sun. I was already in a wheelchair. I didn't want to become blind too.

Mentally I braced myself to rush the robot forward. Even with the robot's asbestos cape for protection, the technicians figured it would not last for more than 30 seconds against the heat.

So that's all I had. Thirty seconds.

If the robot even continued to function once the radiation hit.

The technicians' biggest fear was that the intense radiation would interfere with the robot's computer drive, which received signals from a receiver that was directly linked to a plug in my spinal column, and from there to my brain. I shared that fear. If the robot failed to operate, the nuclear plant would blow. And no one could guess if the radiation interference might scramble the transmissions enough to affect my brain. You see, if a robot is zapped with an electrical current, the controller is knocked unconscious at a minimum, or perhaps even killed. As for radiation interference . . . well, that could be far more deadly.

But with the door three-quarters open, I had no time to worry anymore.

I could see a huge glow through the black glass of my protective shield. Somewhere in the center of it was a rod the length and width of a person's arm. I had to pull it loose before the robot lost its function.

The door stopped opening, then sagged slightly. Had the heat melted its hinges?

I didn't hesitate. My robot was nearly six feet tall, 150 pounds, and incredibly strong. I surged forward, smashing into the door.

Pain instantly shot through me in my wheelchair. The virtual-reality program that enables me to control a robot is so real, it felt like my left arm had broken. I tried to get the robot's left arm to wave. It wouldn't. I'd demolished it against the door.

But the door was open, and I was through.

At the center of the huge glow filling the room was a rod-shaped whiteness almost unbearable to see, even with the black glass that protected the robot's video lenses.

I had to act quickly. The robot already felt sluggish.

I commanded it forward. It lurched, stopped, then lurched again.

Radiation interference!

I'd spent 10 seconds, and the robot was only halfway there.

With all my concentration, I commanded it to continue. Then . . . *clunk.*

It had hit the far end. The core was within reach. All I had to do was somehow get the robot's right arm up and . . .

Another 10 seconds.

The robot's arm began to glow. Would it last long enough to . . . ?

The robot's titanium hand closed on the end of the core rod and fused instantly.

That didn't matter. We'd expected that.

What I had to do now was roll backward and . . .

A sluggishness hit my own brain. Like black glue that oozed into my skull.

Come on, Tyce! I shouted mentally. *Come on! Think!*

In my mind, it felt like I was falling backward. Backward. Backward.

And then the black glue froze all of my thoughts.

Silence squeezed my consciousness into total darkness.

CHAPTER 2

I was startled awake with the feeling of something damp on my forehead.

Opening my eyes, I saw a nurse, probably a little older than my mother. She wiped my forehead with a cool, damp sponge.

Then I remembered. I was in a hospital, somewhere in L.A. I'd woken up late last night as doctors poked and prodded at my body. They had dryly informed me that I was a hero. As my robot had fallen backward, it had pulled the core of uranium far enough out of the sheath to prevent the final stage of uncontrolled nuclear fission. I'd grimaced. With my killer headache, I hadn't felt like a hero. Just like a kid who missed his home. Which for me, of course, was Mars. Then the doctors had given me a painkiller for my headache and let me sleep again.

I guess I'd slept all the way through 'til the next day.

"Good to see you awake," the nurse said. "You gave everybody a scare."

Right now, she was scaring me. The only thing normal about her was the light green nurse's uniform. Her platinum-colored hair was so shiny and piled so high, I knew it had to be a wig. Especially because it wasn't a natural color for a woman with skin darker than chocolate. Her lips were smeared with purple lipstick, and I was ready to choke on the smell of her heavy perfume.

She smiled, showing gleaming white teeth that were surprisingly straight and even. Like she'd spent a lot of money on those teeth but cheaped out on the horrible wig. "Of course, that nuclear plant gave everyone a scare too. What was it like in there?"

"It all happened so fast," I answered, trying not to stare at her bad makeup. I'd never gone trick-or-treating—we never celebrated Halloween on Mars—but I knew about it and wondered if somehow I'd been in a coma so long that it was now October 31.

"Well, I think you were brave," she replied kindly. "Even if you didn't have to go in yourself. That robot . . . you controlled it yourself, right?"

I nodded, wondering if my head would hurt like it had last night. It didn't. I relaxed a little. Weird thing was, something about this nurse looked familiar. Like maybe I'd seen her in a movie from one of the DVD-gigaroms I'd watched growing up on Mars.

I grinned at my strange thoughts. It must be the shock I'd had. I was imagining things. A woman in a wig like this would never be on camera.

"I control the robot with my brain," I answered. No matter how she looked, I reminded myself she was trying to be nice. "Like it's a virtual-reality game. Except I move a real robot, not something in a computer program."

"Wow." A big, encouraging smile again. "Your parents must be proud of you."

She was trying to be nice, so I did my best to hide a frown. *My parents.*

Mom was a plant biologist on Mars, millions and millions of miles away. I missed her badly, along with my friend Rawling, who'd taught me how to control robots when I was a little kid. I wondered what they were doing right now, in another part of the solar system.

As for my dad, Chase Sanders, I didn't even know where he was. Dad was a space pilot. He'd taken the first shuttle to Mars over 15 years earlier. On that eight-month trip he'd met my mom, Kristy Wallace, who was also part of the first expedition of scientists to set up a colony on Mars. They had gotten married as soon as they reached the red planet, and I'd been born almost a year later.

That's why I'd never seen Earth until I came back with Dad on his most recent shuttle from Mars. But something had gone wrong. Dad, my friend Ashley, and I had been arrested almost as soon as we reached the Earth's orbit. We'd been taken to a military prison in the swamps of Florida. But because Dad held some old guy hostage—I found out later he was the Supreme Governor of the World United Federation—Ashley and I had been able to escape the Combat Force prison. Dad had told us to go ahead with our mission—and that we had a six-day countdown to find the pod of kids Ashley had been a part of. Otherwise it would be too late. And then somewhere, in the middle of our mission, we'd heard that Dad had disappeared. No one had heard from him since. Until the nuclear plant thing, he had been my biggest worry. And now—with this nurse's question as a reminder—my worry returned again.

"I'll bet you don't know what your father might think," she said, lowering her voice and leaning forward to whisper, "since you haven't spoken to him since you escaped prison, have you? And you know that he's disappeared. . . ."

Her words had the same effect as if she'd jammed an electric prod into my chest. Only the top people in the Combat Force of the World United Federation knew about my dad. Or that he'd been put in prison as soon as he'd arrived on Earth.

"How do you know about my—"

She put one finger over her lips.

I stopped speaking.

She leaned over farther and put her face up to my ear. She spoke softly as I held my breath, trying not to gag against the smell of her perfume. "There's a reason I'm whispering. You need to assume that electronic devices are set up to listen to whatever you say. To anybody at any time. Not everyone in the Combat Force is on your side."

I pushed my face close to hers. Loose hairs from the platinum wig tickled my nose. "My father?" I asked in a whisper to match hers. "If you know where he is—"

"What I know," she whispered back, "is that the World United Federation won't be able to keep your robot control abilities secret from the world any longer. Not after the nuclear plant."

"My dad. What do you—"

"Even the Terratakers within the Combat Force realized they couldn't put all those millions of lives at risk to protect the secret of this new technology. A hundred lives, sure. A thousand. Maybe even 10,000 lives. But not the entire Los Angeles basin. When it came down to deciding between keeping you under wraps or stopping the blowout, they made the right choice. But that means you are now in great danger."

As if that was news. For the past nine months somebody had been trying to kill me. And I knew the rebel faction, the Terratakers, was involved, because of Dr. Jordan, who had tried to kill Dad, Ashley, and me by sending our shuttle into the sun. The Terratakers had spies everywhere, and they fought hard against the World United Federation. Unlike the Federation, which worked to find solutions for Earth's growing population, such as making planets like Mars suitable for humans, the Terratakers were a terrorist organization that worked against the colonization of Mars. Instead they claimed the Earth's population should be reduced. Fewer babies should be born. And when humans had outlived their usefulness, they should be put to sleep.

What the Terratakers believed was pretty scary. Because if you followed what they believed, it meant I wouldn't be alive. To them someone in a wheelchair with useless legs isn't worth enough to use valuable water and food.

"My dad—" I insisted. It seemed weird enough to be a dream. All of our conversation was in a low whisper. Although this woman had on enough makeup to be a clown, I had no choice but to take her seriously because of what she knew.

"Remember, the Combat Force has too many Terrataker traitors inside it. That's why they were almost able to storm the Summit of Governors."

The Summit of Governors! Where all the world leaders gathered each year to deal with international problems.

She straightened and stared at me to see if I understood what it meant that she knew about the Summit. The surprise on my face must have shown.

"I know," she whispered, leaning forward again. "The attempt on the governors' lives was supposed to be a secret too. You can't imagine the steps the Combat Force took to bury that. And the danger of robot soldiers controlled by an army of kids. Except now they'll decide to show you off to the world. And put you at great risk."

"You can't know this!" The Summit of Governors in New York City had been meeting to talk about whether or not to continue the funding of the Mars Project: the colonization of Mars. And it had come within 30 seconds of ending with all the leaders being shot by robot soldiers controlled by the Terrataker faction. Yet the world didn't know about it. The newspapers had reported the commotion around the Summit as a Hollywood stunt for the promotion of an upcoming movie. To the public, it was as if nothing had happened.

"I do know this. Which should tell you that all the rest of what I'm telling you is true."

"My dad. What about—"

Someone knocked at the door. It was another nurse. Much younger, with spiked red hair and a nose ring.

"Hello?" The red-haired nurse seemed confused. "This is my room on the duty chart," she said to the older nurse at my bed. "I didn't know another shift had started."

The nurse in front of me straightened out the sheets of my bed. "Obviously there's been a mistake. Why don't you check at the front desk?"

"But—"

"Don't mess with me, girl. Just go to the front desk and make sure you got that duty chart right," the platinum blonde nurse said. She'd been talking to me in a normal voice. Talking to this new nurse, suddenly her voice was high and whiny to match the way she looked. Who *was* this woman with the bad lipstick?

"OK," the red-haired nurse said after a second. "I'll be right back." We could hear the soft sound of her shoes padding down the hallway.

"Time to go," my perfumed nurse said. Her voice was normal again. "And remember what I said."

I wanted to know about my dad. "Don't go," I pleaded.

We heard the distant sounds of shoes in the hallway. Headed our way from the front desk.

"Can't stay," she said simply.

And with that, she was gone. Whoever she was.

Gone. With whatever else she knew.

CHAPTER 3

A tall, broad-shouldered man nodded at me and sat down beside my bed. A man in Combat Force uniform. General Jeb McNamee, known as "Cannon," had a face ugly enough to scare little children—a square face, bent nose, and shaved head. He was the kind of man you wanted on your side.

Listening devices, the mysterious nurse had said.

If they were here, it wasn't because of this military man. After all, he had sent Nate, who'd been part of Cannon's elite unit in the Combat Force called the E.A.G.L.E.S. And Nate had helped Ashley and me flee the Florida Everglades. Then Cannon himself had helped us find and rescue the pod of robot kids in Arizona. But was the nurse in the hospital right? Could no one be trusted? Did the infiltration of the Terratakers extend even to people like Cannon, who seemed to be on my side?

"Good to see you bright-eyed," the general said in his gruff voice. "For a while there, I thought we'd be giving you a 21-gun salute."

"Twenty-one-gun salute?"

"A military tradition. An honor at funeral ceremonies.

Twenty-one shots fired in the air. The total of one and seven and seven and six. It started as an American tradition, and now all the Federation military in the world follow the custom."

He squinted at me to see if I would figure it out.

"One seven seven six," I repeated slowly. "Seventeen seventy-six." I got it. And grinned. "The year the United States declared its independence from England."

"Yes, sir," Cannon said. "Glad to see your brains are still intact." He patted my shoulder.

Terrataker traitors are everywhere in the military. But I can trust Cannon, I told myself. Yet I didn't like the little bit of doubt in the back of my mind.

I could hear my mom's words now. They'd been drilled into my brain: *Tyce, in times of crisis, people will fail you. But God never will. You can trust him. Then he'll show you who you can trust.*

So I sent up a silent prayer, hoping for a quick answer. No answer came, but instead a deep peace.

Yes, I decided, I would trust Cannon. After all, Chad, his own son, was still among some of the missing kids who had been kidnapped at a young age to be operated on for robot control. And, in searching for his son, Cannon had been the main person responsible for stopping the Summit of Governors assassination attempt. He'd helped save my life.

Surely he couldn't be one of the high-level traitors inside the World United Federation's Combat Force.

I wanted to tell Cannon about the strange woman. *But if there were listening devices . . .*

My dad was out there. Somewhere, needing help.

To be on the safe side, I decided to wait to tell Cannon about the nurse with the strange message. Or about the red-haired nurse coming back and saying no other nurse was supposed to be on duty. That had convinced me the strange message hadn't come from a real nurse, but someone dressed up to look like a nurse. Who was she, really? That question burned inside me.

"Tyce, I've got some exciting news," Cannon said.

"My father?"

"Not yet. But don't worry. We have the resources of the entire Combat Force at our disposal," he assured me. Then he continued. "It's about Mars. Now it looks like we can push the colonization schedule ahead by 50 years."

"Fifty years! That might save millions of lives!"

My heart started to pound with excitement. Mom and Rawling would love to hear this, if they hadn't already. After all, they'd been working for that very thing for the past 15 years. The establishment of a dome under which people could live on Mars was only Phase 1 of a long-term plan. Phase 2, which the Mars colony was now in, was to grow plant hybrids outside the dome so that more oxygen could be added to the atmosphere. The long-range plan—which could take over 100 years—was to make the entire planet a place for humans to live outside the dome.

People on Earth desperately needed the room. Already the planet had too few resources for the many people on it. If Mars could be made a new colony, then Earth could start shipping people there to live. If not, new wars might begin, and millions and millions of people would die from war or starvation or disease. Even now countries verged on war because of the diminishing amount of resources.

"Fifty years," Cannon repeated. "And the irony is that we'll be using a method that would never be welcome on Earth. Pollution. At least, pollution in the form of carbon dioxide."

I listened as Cannon explained. On Earth, too much carbon dioxide caused *the greenhouse effect.* Light from the sun entered the Earth's atmosphere and was not able to bounce back into outer space. Carbon dioxide trapped heat. That was not good on Earth, but on the cold planet of Mars, it would be great. Yes, most of the atmosphere of Mars already consisted of carbon dioxide. But there wasn't enough atmosphere. If billions of tons more could be added, then finally Mars would start absorbing heat.

"Scientists have had the plans in place for building the generators and even for shipping them in pieces to Mars. But until now it was impossible to assemble them except at too great a cost."

"Carbon-dioxide generators." I imagined clouds of white gas mushrooming and vanishing on the barren surface of the red planet. Mushrooming and mushrooming for years and years. And plants could live in the thickening atmosphere, breathing in carbon dioxide and releasing oxygen that wouldn't drift into outer space because finally there would be enough atmosphere to hold it.

"What's truly made this possible is you," Cannon continued. "You in particular. And all the others with robot-control abilities. Let me explain."

Again, I listened.

"Because there are enough kids like you, who can volunteer to assemble the generators easily on the surface of Mars. Technicians need bulky space suits, which can rip far too easily. Kids safe inside the dome, though, can handle robots outside the dome. Robots that don't need air or water. Those robots can work 100 times faster than humans. We can get the generators up and running in a matter of months. Kids who volunteer will be amply repaid by the government. The important thing now is that Tyce

Sanders gets support from all Earth countries to undertake this next phase."

"Me?" I asked, stunned.

"This will sound cold, Tyce. But you are the perfect public-relations opportunity. Many of the highest-ranking Combat Force officials were determined to keep robot control a secret as long as possible. They were afraid the world would see only the negatives. Especially if they found out about the soldier robots. But now they can see the positives. We are going to introduce you to the world as the hero you are. And people won't be afraid of robot control."

It was strange. Throughout my life I'd always thought of myself as just a kid. A kid in a wheelchair. And now the very thing that had put me in a wheelchair—the surgery-gone-wrong that had inserted a plug in my spine so that I could control robots—made me a hero. Weird. Well, I guess it was true what Mom always said: God does use our disabilities for good.

The words of the mysterious nurse came back to me. *The attempt on the governors' lives was supposed to be a secret too. You can't imagine the steps the Combat Force took to bury that. And the danger of robot soldiers controlled by an army of kids. Except now they'll decide to show you off to the world. And put you at great risk.*

What she predicted was happening right now.

It was almost as if Cannon had read my suspicious thoughts—thoughts I didn't want to have about him.

"I apologize," he said. "In a way, we are using you. I hope you'll allow that, however. We desperately need approval of robot control in public-opinion polls all over the world. With that approval, politicians will support the next phase of Mars development. Without it, opposition will ground us. And the Terratakers will win."

"I'll do what I can to help," I finally said.

"Thank you." He spoke with dignity. "We'll immediately set up a media conference at the World United Federation Center in New York. And after that . . ."

I waited. I didn't like the concern etched into Cannon's face.

". . . I think you'll need to go to the Moon. There's that last pod of missing kids. They need our help."

"Yes, sir," I agreed.

"There's more. Lots more."

"Sir?"

He stood. "The doctors tell me you're ready to go. Let me explain the rest of it on the way back to New York."

CHAPTER 4

"Tantalum."

"I beg your pardon, sir?"

It had taken barely a half hour to get in the air. A helicopter had flown us from the hospital to the runway, where a jet waited. So Cannon and I now sat in a military jet, traveling 30,000 feet above the ground, headed back to New York at 600 miles an hour. The shades on the windows had been pulled down, and a projector was set up between us.

"It's a rare metal," he answered from the darkness. "So rare and precious that it shouldn't be a surprise that kids like you have been put into slavery to mine it."

Slavery. Kids like me. Able to control robots. But unlike me, unable to control anything else in their lives.

"Let me back up a second." He clicked a button on his remote, and a photo of the Moon's surface appeared on a screen in front of us. At least I guessed it was the Moon. In the darkness beyond it was the familiar blue-and-white ball of Earth that I had watched so often from a telescope on Mars. In the foreground of the photo, beyond small craters of the gray soil, was a platform buggy about to enter a low, flat building.

"In its purest form, tantalum is a rare gray-white metal. Melting point at about 3,000 degrees Celsius, and boiling point at well over 5,000 degrees Celsius. Pure tantalum is extremely flexible. It can be drawn into microscopically thin wires. At normal temperatures, it's almost impossible to corrode with any acid. Its chief use is in computer components."

"I think I understand," I said. The hum of the jet engines forced me to raise my voice. "Computers are everywhere, so if tantalum is rare . . ."

"Exactly. The more computers, the more it is needed. The more it is needed, the more it is worth. Right now, it has about 100 times the value of gold. Historically, it was mined in Africa and Canada. Those mines are basically depleted. But major deposits were recently discovered on the Moon. In the sector controlled by the Manchurians."

"The Manchurian Sector . . ." I knew some history. Manchuria was a province in China. Although the area itself had not expanded over the last 50 years, its political influence had gone far beyond China.

General Cannon clicked his remote again. A new photo flashed onto the screen. This one was not of the surface of the Moon. It was an interior shot—I guessed the inside of the building in the photo before. It was like a large warehouse. Lights hung from overhead. Men in space suits tended to a platform buggy. But in the background were . . .

Another click brought the background closer and into full focus.

Robots! Just like the one I controlled. I didn't have to say it. Cannon wouldn't be showing me this unless it meant the pod of missing kids was involved.

"Once again, let me back up," the general said. "You probably know enough about Earth politics to understand that each country within the World United Federation is independent."

"Yes," I said. "But the world population crisis forced the countries to work closer together and form an alliance. Just like different states within the United States work together. But the Terratakers wanted to make sure that didn't happen." I shivered slightly.

Cannon leaned toward me. "I want to let you in on a military reality and the war no one will admit is being fought," he said. "Publicly it's believed that the Terratakers consist of individuals from each country who believe in a cause. Much like the environmentalists of the previous century."

"It's not true?"

"No," the general grimly answered. I strained to hear over the noise of the jet. "When the World United Federation formed, there were two military superpowers that balanced each other—the United States and China. Late in the 20th century, the Russians fell by the wayside as their economy collapsed. As Russia fell, China stepped into the vacuum and began to dominate until it almost rivaled the United States. It was a peaceful rivalry, until the Manchurians came to power."

"A political base in China that defied their country's mandate of world trade," I said. "It divided China into pro- and anti-American rivalries. And then rebels within other countries across the world began to identify with the Manchurian movement. The World United Federation is not allowed to interfere with internal difficulties of any country. The Manchurians won a brief civil war within China and now call the shots there."

I grinned at Cannon's raised eyebrows. "Hey, homeschooling is a big deal on Mars. And I was the only student on the planet. So I had to learn everything."

Cannon grinned back, then got serious. "To both China and the U.S., the goals of the World United Federation are far too important to risk open war. Yet beneath the surface, the Americans are locked in battle against the Manchurian movement for dominance. It's like the Cold War that took place between the United States and Russia for 45 years after World War II. We have our spies. They have theirs. And if the Terratakers succeed, it will shift the balance of power to the Manchurians."

"You're saying the Terratakers are backed by the Manchurians?"

"Exactly," Cannon said. "And all the other countries that would openly side with the Manchurians if they ever thought the Americans would be defeated in a world war."

"I think I understand," I said. "Publicly, all countries stay in line with the World United Federation because of the power of the United States. But all the ones waiting for the slightest chance are working with the Manchurians. And now you're telling me the Manchurians and Terratakers . . ."

"The Manchurians didn't form the Terrataker political movement. But once it happened, the Manchurians took advantage of the terrorist organization. After all, they already shared some of the Terratakers' philosophy on population control: to limit the number of children a family could have. And they had openly supported the United States' Human Genome Project, which began in 1990."

"The Genome Project?" I asked, curious.

"It began as a way to identify genes and map human DNA, so that humans would know if they were carrying a genetic disease or not. But soon it was being used to identify and convict criminals and to test not-yet-born babies for genetic defects. Now scientists in the Terrataker camp are arguing that everyone in the world should be routinely tested and the results kept on file. It frightens me to think of how they might use that information—to abort any babies with genetic defects, for example." The general cleared his throat. "Yet we can't openly accuse the Manchurians of supporting the Terratakers. It would be too easy for them to deny it, and too easy for them to use those charges to swing world opinion in their favor. But we know it's happening. For example, Luke Daab and Dr. Jordan—"

"Terrataker agents! You mean they're not only running this robot-control program, but with Manchurian help?"

"Yes," the general said calmly. "Without the money and resources made available to them by a military superpower, those two men wouldn't have been able to accomplish anything. Instead . . ."

General Cannon didn't have to say more about that. Both men had come very close to killing me on Mars and on the return from Mars. Both men had engineered the assassination attempt at the Summit of Governors.

"Let me put it this way, Tyce. In the end, whoever controls Mars will control the power on Earth." The general paused.

That was a pretty scary thought. With the Terratakers in control, human life would become disposable. Like diapers. People like me with disabilities wouldn't be around. Old people would be killed. Babies with genetic defects wouldn't be allowed to be born.

My brain spun with the possibilities. The kind of DNA you had could control whether you lived or died, your right to attend college or university, even what job you were allowed to have. . . . A simple doctor's test of your DNA could determine not only your life, but the quality and length of your life. But did other humans have the right to choose what was really in God's hands?

"Within the Federation," Cannon continued, "the United States government is working hard to keep the Mars Project a neutral one, governed by all countries. But the Terratakers want to have it all to themselves. It's a strange balancing act in public perception. On the surface the Terratakers seem passionately opposed to space exploration and expansion. But what they really oppose is Federation control of the planet. They want it for themselves. The Manchurians want it to publicly appear as if they support Federation control of Mars, but secretly they want it for themselves too. Because if they ever gain control of Mars and its resources, they will openly try to take over the Federation on Earth. And if that happens, the solar system will be theirs. That's why the Terratakers and Manchurians are so willing to work together. The Manchurians have structure and political control but must keep a respectable appearance. The Terratakers have a dirty reputation and are willing to do the dirty work, but they need the power and resources of the Manchurians."

I kept staring at the photo that showed robots beneath a warehouse building on the Moon. "If the warehouse on the Moon is in the Manchurian Sector, that means it's protected, right?"

"According to Federation structure, yes. Countries have individual rights. On Earth, the Manchurian military can't enter the United States without permission. Nor can they enter our sector on the Moon. The same is true, of course, in reverse. Their sector has total immunity, which extends even to their orbit stations in space. It's a prime example of how the Manchurians are able to help the Terratakers."

General Cannon clicked again. The next photo showed an extreme close-up of a robot.

"Some time ago a Federation agent managed to sneak in as a worker and send these photos by satellite. But we're guessing he was caught. At least we haven't heard from him since. At the time, we thought China had extremely sophisticated robots. But now, because of you, we know better. The only thing that makes sense is that the robots are controlled by human brains."

"So that's why you think the last pod of kids are on the Moon?" I thought of what I'd seen four days ago in Arizona for the first time. Kids trapped in huge jelly tubes, in 24-hour-a-day life support. Unable to move and hooked to computers under the control of Dr. Jordan.

"I can't answer that," Cannon said. "All we know for sure about the operation is what the public knows. Great quantities of tantalum are shipped from the Manchurian Sector on the Moon to Earth. That means massive amounts of money are transferred to the Manchurian coalition, which in turn is able to finance more Terrataker action against the Federation. This money has also attracted other countries to unofficially back the Manchurians. We're talking far more than a China power base."

He scratched his head. "And the worst part is that we have no way of proving our theory: that those robots are controlled by the last pod of kids. We can't get into that warehouse. But if we could prove to the world what's happening, the Manchurians will lose most of their support."

He paused. "I believe my son is among those slaves. So what I'm about to ask is for more than the Federation. It's for me personally. Tyce, will you go into that warehouse in the Manchurian Sector and bring us back the proof we need to help those kids?"

29

CHAPTER 5

Pop! Pop! Pop!

Although the blinding light made no sound, my head hurt so badly it seemed like I could hear each flash from each camera. I'd only been back in New York for less than a day, and I hadn't been out of the hospital long enough.

Pop! Pop! Pop!

Cannon kept a hand on my shoulder, walking beside me as I rolled my wheelchair toward dozens of photographers gathered below the front of the enormous stage for the morning's press conference. Boom mikes hung in the air above them. Television cameras were mounted on each side.

"You're right," I told Cannon.

"Right?"

"When you said that they look like a—"

He squeezed my shoulder hard. "Not here. You never know what their recording equipment will pick up."

I'd been about to say they looked like a pack of hungry jackals. Because, of course, that had been the general's description in the back room five minutes earlier as we went over the news conference material.

"You ready?" the general asked in a low voice. "We can always turn back. Even now."

We neared the front of the stage. A set of microphones had been placed at a lower level so I could answer questions directly from my wheelchair.

I was tempted to turn back. How could anybody be ready for this? Cannon had explained that the conference was about to be broadcast live on every major television network in the world. With translations from English into every other major language. I was about to be presented as the first human born on Mars. Someone who could control robots by a hookup to his brain. Billions of people were about to see every nervous twitch and hear every nervous stutter. Both the mysterious nurse and the general had warned me that my life would never be the same after this.

Soon the world would know about robot control. The secret would be out. Would it be worth the risk to me personally? I wondered. Yet somehow I couldn't help but hope that letting the secret out to the world would buy my father's safety and allow him to come out of hiding. If what the nurse had said was true and he was alive.

"I'm ready," I said.

We reached the microphones as murmuring grew louder among the dozens of media people. Lights kept flashing from different cameras.

"Ladies and gentlemen," Cannon began in his deep voice, "I will begin with a prepared statement. Any questions following will be directed to me first. Those that I find suitable I will allow Tyce Sanders to answer."

"Why not let him decide for himself?" a raspy voice called. It came from a skinny man with a wispy gray beard who wore a tweed sport coat with blue jeans. "We heard rumors he's the reason the nuclear plant didn't blow. Like he's some kind of freak!"

The general smiled at the man. But it was a cold smile, and I was glad it wasn't directed at me. When he pointed at the man who had shouted out, a soldier walked up to the man, tapped him on the shoulder, and then escorted him out of the room.

"As you might guess," Cannon said as the door closed, "I intend for this to be a civilized event. Tyce hasn't spent much time on Earth. So we *will* be respectful of him and make his transition into public life as dignified as possible. Am I clear?"

Silence hung among the group of grown men and women, as if the general were a strict teacher addressing a classroom of young children.

"Thank you," the general said after a weighty pause. "Let me begin."

Reaching inside his jacket, he pulled out a pair of glasses and placed them carefully on his face. Then he leaned forward and read from a sheet on the podium in front of him.

"As you all know, two days ago a nuclear plant near Los Angeles, California, came within a half hour of catastrophic meltdown. Millions of lives were at stake. Millions more would have been affected for generations by the DNA mutations and cancer of radiation poisoning. The environmental disaster would have been one of this century's greatest tragedies. Yet the meltdown did not happen. I know there has been intense media curiosity on how the disaster was prevented. Today you will get the answer."

Murmuring began again, growing louder and louder.

Cannon waited, as if he knew there was no way to prevent the murmuring.

I'd read some of the headlines. Little had been revealed to the public yet. The Combat Force officials had decided to wait until they knew I was in good enough health to hold this conference.

Cannon resumed speaking into the microphone. "Essentially we were able to send a robot into a situation where no human would have survived. And at the same time, we were able to send a human in where no normal robot would have had the intelligence or flexibility to handle the situation. How did we do both at the same time?"

Another pause.

"This young man in front of you is able to control a robot with a hookup that links his brain and a computer. The computer in turn transmits his brain waves to the robot, so that it moves the way a body moves as commanded by the brain. The computer also sends information from the robot back to his brain. In short, it is virtual reality taken one step further."

Now the murmuring became open, excited conversation among the media members. I understood. It had only been a little over nine months since I'd known about robot control myself, even though I'd practiced virtual-reality simulations as far back as I could remember.

"Our press secretary will give you handouts at the end of the conference," the general said. "These handouts detail many of the technical aspects involved in robot control. Let me say now, however, that it took old-fashioned human courage for this young man to prevent the nuclear plant meltdown. And to counter any critics of this new technology, let me be very quick to add that this is the philosophy of the World United Federation's approach to robot control. The robots themselves are no different than any other tool we use—from a hammer to an airplane. It is the human behind it who matters."

General Cannon stopped to take a drink of water from a glass under the podium. Then he removed his glasses, folded them neatly, and slipped them back into his pocket.

"And now," he said, "let me introduce to you the first human born on Mars. Tyce Sanders."

With that, the eyes of the entire world turned upon me.

CHAPTER 6

I did what any normal human would do in front of billions of people.

I froze. Except for a smile that felt like someone was putting a finger in each side of my mouth and pulling. I didn't know if I was supposed to speak, so I just kept smiling at the reporters. I hoped I didn't have any particles hanging out of my nose.

"General, with all due respect to Tyce Sanders," one reporter said, "we can plainly see he is in a wheelchair. Was this a result of the nuclear plant accident? Did anything go wrong during his handling of the robot? Was he injured as a result?"

"No, it wasn't the result of the nuclear plant accident," Cannon stated. "No, nothing went wrong during his robot control. And no, he wasn't injured as a result."

That was true in one way. But in another way, I *was* in a wheelchair because of robot control. For when the pioneer operation had been done to my spine to allow the computer hookup to my nervous system, something had gone wrong. And because it took place on Mars, the doctor didn't have access to the specialized equipment he needed to fix the mistake immediately. That mistake left me in my wheelchair. I couldn't remember ever walking or running. It used to make me angry. But I was slowly learning how to live with it.

"Yet we heard he was hurt," another reporter said. Her white-blonde hair and red dress stood out from the pack. "We heard he's been in a hospital and—"

"Recovering from an exhausting rescue effort," Cannon said. "Tyce is in perfect health. Just tired."

"General," a taller man said, "I would guess until today this has been top secret. How much money has been spent on this robot-control research?" He chewed on his pencil while waiting for a response.

"It's in the report."

"Did the Federation approve this money, and if so, why wasn't it subject to public debate?" the man threw in quickly.

Cannon had warned me this type of question would arise. He took it without flinching. "Surely you understand that every government has issues of national security. This was one of them."

"Did Tyce Sanders have a choice in the operation?" the pencil chewer asked.

For a moment, Cannon paused. It was a moment too long. Because his brief silence said everything. I had not had a choice.

"The operation that allows the spinal hookup to a computer must be done before the child is three years old," Cannon said slowly. "Otherwise the neuron connections won't grow into place. We had the consent of his mother, who is involved in the Mars Project."

I coughed discreetly. Cannon looked at me.

"May I answer?" I whispered.

The general nodded.

Barely enough moisture remained in my mouth to swallow back my nervousness. What would I say in my first words to the world?

"Because of the operation, I am able to see and hear worlds that no human has ever been able to explore. Outer space. The surface of Mars. I don't think there's a person alive who wouldn't want to have the chances I've been given as a result."

There was more to say, but I kept it to myself, because it was private. . . .

Dad had been off on a flight to Earth when my mom had to make the decision. Because the Mars Project hadn't counted on babies in its early stages, my mom was given a choice. Either she could send me back to Earth on a spaceship and risk what the G-forces would do to a baby, or she could allow me to have the operation and stay with her on Mars. So she made the best choice she could. No one guessed that something would go wrong during the surgery and that my legs would be paralyzed as a result. What's helped me deal with it is knowing in the last while that there's a God and that even when things look bad, he's still in control. He can make good things happen from bad things. Like the ability to travel the universe through controlling a robot with my brain. . . .

"General! General!" an African-American woman in black pants and a black sweater interrupted.

"Yes, Ms. Borris . . ."

Ms. Borris!

Earlier Cannon had told me that Ms. Evangeline Borris was the most feared reporter in New York City. As a young reporter, she'd broken a story that overthrew a presidency. She was a legend now, and not even that old, Cannon had said grimly. But Cannon had not described her to me. And when I saw her now, I gripped the arms of my wheelchair and tried to hold back my surprise.

It was her! Put on the platinum wig, smear lipstick across the lower part of her face, and it was the mysterious nurse who had visited me in the hospital! Only now she was the picture of dignity.

She spoke calmly. "If this young man can control a robot capable of going places humans can't, wouldn't he make an ideal soldier?"

A hush fell on the reporters. They all looked at the general.

"He is not a soldier, Ms. Borris," Cannon answered.

"Are there others like him?" she asked.

"Ms. Borris," he said firmly, "for reasons of national security, I cannot—"

"Can you tell us about an incident on 04.01.2040 at the World United Federation Summit of Governors?" she persisted.

My guess was that only someone like Ms. Borris dared interrupt the general, for he didn't give her the same cold, hard stare he'd given the man who had been escorted out. Instead he seemed to squirm.

"And can you confirm or deny rumors that robot soldiers were involved in an assassination attempt?"

"Unlike you," Cannon said, biting back his anger, "I am not in the business of selling rumors to the public. Again, for reasons of national security, I cannot confirm or deny."

Muttering grew rapidly through the crowd, moving like a wave of water. Cannon had not denied it. And I guessed Ms. Borris was not known for asking questions unless she had a good source. To all the reporters, then, the general's refusal to answer said a lot.

"And lastly!" Ms. Borris now had to shout to be heard. When the others realized she wasn't finished, they quieted instantly. "General, is it true that children have been forced into robot control as slaves in a tantalum mine on the Moon?"

"Ms. Borris," the general said, the intensity of his voice like a whip crack, "I thought a respected reporter like you would not have to stoop to creating your own headlines to sell newspapers."

"Yes or no, General," she insisted. "Child slavery? If a child like Tyce Sanders is able to control a robot, who controls the child? And who controls those who control the child? Especially if the interests of national security make it so possible to keep this secret?"

The general drew a deep breath. "Interesting speculation, Ms. Borris. Perhaps you might be on the verge of a new career as a fiction author?"

"Hardly," she snapped back. "Not when this is far more bizarre than fiction. My sources tell me—"

She didn't get a chance to finish.

Without warning, four soldiers stampeded through the middle of the crowd, shoving reporters in all directions. Without hesitation those soldiers leaped upon the stage. Two of them grabbed me out of my wheelchair. The other two yanked the wheelchair away and began running with it.

I watched helplessly as they sprinted toward the nearest exit. My feet dangled off the ground as the two soldiers held me by the arms.

"Hey," I said to the nearest soldier. "What's the—"

"Not a word in front of the cameras," the soldier growled. He leaned forward and whispered in my ear. "There's a bomb. In your wheelchair."

The wheelchair they had run with.

Ten seconds later a loud boom from outside shook the entire room.

CHAPTER 7

"Tyce, what do you think we're up against?"

This came from Cannon. He and I were in a huge Combat Force helicopter, skimming along the Atlantic shoreline as we flew from New York City to Washington, D.C., where I was supposed to meet with Ashley before we moved to a Moon shuttle launch site in Florida. The roar of the engines was far too loud for us to talk without help of the headsets both of us wore. The vibrations of the helicopter engines rumbled through my body as I answered the general's question.

"We're up against someone wanting me dead," I said. Only a half hour had passed since soldiers had whisked all of us out of the media conference center. I was still shaky. I sat in a new wheelchair, taken from a hospital. It had no electric motor. And it seemed far too heavy with Earth gravity.

"What else?" Cannon said.

"There's your son," I answered. "He's still missing. I know you want to find him."

Cannon nodded. Beyond his large square head, I saw the endless blue of the ocean through the window of the helicopter. All I had to do was turn the other way to see the green and brown of the shoreline, with the ribbons of highway and an occasional inland city.

"I want my son," the general said. There was a catch in his voice. "Nothing is truer than that. Just like each of the robot kids wants to find his or her parents."

It hadn't been that long since Cannon had discovered his son was still alive. Although it appeared he'd drowned in a boating accident, Chad's body had never been found. Then one day a stranger had walked up to the general on the street and told him that Chad was alive and being held hostage. Once Cannon found out about the robot control, he assumed the robot-control operation had been done to his son too. Just like it had been done to hundreds of other kids across the world, all kidnapped in situations that made it look like deaths where the bodies couldn't be found. And each of those kids was a child of a high-ranking politician, World United Federation official, or Combat Force general. Twenty-four kids made up each group, called a *pod,* and there were 10 pods total. Nine of the pods of kids had been rescued. But when they arrived at the location of the 10th pod, the jelly tubes were empty. Those were the kids who were probably on the Moon, held hostage to do tantalum mining.

"Yet," Cannon said, interrupting my thoughts, "this is even bigger than what matters to you or me. Or for that matter, to all the other robot-control kids."

The nine pods of rescued kids were now safe in the mountain retreat in Parker, Arizona. There the Combat Force was conducting DNA tests on their blood samples to help match them to their parents. Most of the kids were still in shock, for it was only recently they'd found out their parents were alive. They'd assumed they were orphans. Ashley too. She could have had the DNA test in D.C. but wanted the chance to be with some of her pod brothers and sisters before she went to the Moon with me to look for the last pod.

As I was thinking this, Cannon stopped speaking, as if he, too, were lost in thought.

I let my eyes drift to the horizon of endless ocean. It fascinated me. All that water, when on Mars there was nothing. No water. Which meant no life. Why was it that Earth had that one-in-a-hundred-billion-billion-billion chance that led to the right combination of sunlight and water and oxygen that allowed life? Most of my life involved science of one sort or another so I thought about this a lot. Some people believe this happened through random chance. But for me, the more I learned about science, the more it pointed me toward God.

"Tyce."

I looked at Cannon.

"I wish I could tell you more of what's happening," he said.

"What's happening?"

He looked sad, tired. "There's some unfair stuff that I . . ." He took a breath. "Look, about the bomb. Don't worry. All right?"

"But it was a big bomb. Bad bomb. Like blow-up-and-make-lots-of-noise bomb. I—"

"Don't worry. That's all I can say."

This is what he'd been thinking about? That I shouldn't be afraid of bombs? Before I could say anything else, our pilot interrupted.

"Sir." Our pilot tapped his own headset. "There's an incoming call for you to take."

"Excuse me," Cannon said. Then he switched to a different channel and began speaking into his headset.

I thought of Ms. Borris. How did she know what she did? And that led me to thinking about her question about kids as slaves. Of anyone in the world, Ashley and I knew what that meant, for we'd seen it firsthand in the kids in the jelly tubes in Parker, Arizona. Even more than that, Ashley herself had been part of the Arizona pod before Dr. Jordan forced her to go with him to Mars for the deadly Hammerhead torpedo mission.

Suddenly the roar of the helicopter's engines seemed to drop. *Strange,* I thought. *We're still above the water.* The D.C. base wasn't anywhere in sight.

Then my stomach rose to my throat. The helicopter had just pitched straight sideways!

Wind hit my face.

I looked away from the general and saw that the pilot's door was wide open. With the pilot gone!

Then the roar of the engines stopped completely.

With all the power off, the helicopter began to fall toward the ocean!

CHAPTER 8

There it was. Our helicopter. Tumbling. Tumbling. And at the last minute, just above the water, straightening. And leveling.

On television, it didn't look real. But seeing it—even from the safety of my wheelchair in a secure room on the D.C. Combat Force base—brought back to me the horror of thinking we were about to hit the water at well over 100 miles an hour.

"Wow," Ashley said from her chair beside me. "Heaven's going to be a great place. But let me be selfish here. I'm just glad you're not there yet."

It *was* good to be alive. And good to be with the only friend my age I had. Ashley was a year younger than me, nearly 14. With her short, straight black hair and almond-shaped eyes that squinted when she grinned, she looked like a tomboy. But when her face was serious, she could have been a model from the cover of a magazine.

Although Ashley and I had only met a little over nine months ago when she'd arrived on my dad's shuttle to Mars, we had become close friends quickly. We'd been through a lot together in that short amount of time. I could really trust her, and she trusted me. She, too, loved looking through the telescope on Mars, and it was those evenings that we'd talked a lot about God and the fact that he'd created an awesome universe.

"Wow is right," I agreed. Even though it was the next morning, I could still feel the sensation of falling toward death.

The television announcer's voice broke in as the clip of the tumbling helicopter ran twice more. "Although General Jeb McNamee, known as 'Cannon' by his military comrades, had not been behind the controls of a helicopter for more than 20 years, he was able to avoid what would have been certain death for himself and Tyce Sanders. It is speculated that the pilot who abandoned the helicopter parachuted down to a waiting boat. Neither the pilot nor the boat have been found, but authorities are certain this assassination attempt is linked to the Terratakers, the worldwide terrorist group that reflects much of the world's opposition to outer-space expansion. This was the second attempt in one day to assassinate Tyce Sanders."

There was a quick close-up of me looking into the camera, taken at the media conference yesterday, before the bomb blew. I was grateful not to see anything hanging from my nose. But I hated the goofy smile I wore.

"Reaction around the world shows mounting sympathy for the World United Federation's Combat Force, a military organization that, until now, few people seemed to like. But when the Terratakers try to kill a teenager, it should be no surprise that they lose some of their popular support. Now to New York, where our network political analyst has this to say."

The screen immediately showed a serious man in a three-piece navy blue suit, holding a clipboard.

"Yes, Fred. As our viewers probably know by now, the

first assassination attempt occurred less than an hour earlier yesterday at a news conference in New York City. There Combat Force officials had just announced to the world the incredible ability of Tyce Sanders to handle a robot by hooking up his brain to the robot's computer. As if this unveiling of technology that fuses human with machine wasn't enough to get the world's attention, it was also announced that Tyce Sanders had controlled the robot that prevented a nuclear plant meltdown outside of Los Angeles earlier in the week."

The analyst's image faded as the network logo appeared on the screen. A deep voice said: "Robot control. Colonization of Mars. And terrorist assassination attempts. More on this when our one-hour special returns . . ."

The television image switched quickly to two women in business suits. One sniffed under her armpit, hoping the other wouldn't notice. But the other woman did notice and began to recommend a brand of deodorant.

"Strange planet you live on," I mentioned to Ashley. "Life or death situations on the news. With breaks to bring us really important things, like controlling body odor before important meetings."

"I've been meaning to talk to you about that serious issue," she said, grinning and plugging her nose. "Now what was the name of that deodorant you could use so badly?"

"Hah, hah."

We were interrupted by the opening of the door.

Cannon moved into the room. "I'm sorry I had to leave you two alone for so long," he apologized. "But I knew you would be safe here."

Then he paused and sat down next to Ashley.

I knew something was up just from the way he sat down.

"Ashley," he said slowly and kindly, totally unlike his normally brusque self, "I have some news for you. The computers have been humming 24/7. They now have a match to the results of your DNA tests."

"My parents?" Her voice trembled.

He nodded.

Ashley's eyes widened, and she turned her head to look at me.

I was as startled as she was. After all, Ashley had spent her entire life thinking she was an orphan and had only recently been told by Dr. Jordan that her parents were alive. Now we knew it was true.

The look in her eyes was a mix of fear and excitement. *What will they be like?* it seemed to say.

My stomach fluttered nervously for her. What would it be like to find out you had parents after all these years? And to finally meet them? And then another thought struck me. *Will it change Ashley's and my friendship? What if her parents don't want her to return to Mars? Or she decides to stay with them and not go?*

"Ashley? You OK?" the general asked.

Ashley just nodded.

"They're here right now, ready to meet you," the general continued.

He stood up, stepped toward the door, and opened it.

I could tell Ashley was holding her breath.

A man and a woman stepped into the room. They looked approximately my parents' ages. The man was of medium height, with thick, dark curly hair. He looked stiff in tan pants and a golf shirt. The woman was petite and Asian like Ashley. She wore a red hat that matched her dress. Her eyes looked misty, as if she'd been crying.

They ignored me and stared at Ashley. They smiled, but with hesitation, as if they weren't quite sure how to react.

"Ashley, please say hello to your parents," Cannon said.

CHAPTER 9

Late night 04.05.2040

Before, I thought I was lonely. Before, when I remembered Mars and my mom there and how she and my friend Rawling McTigre were millions and millions of miles away. Before, when I hoped and prayed my dad was OK wherever he was. But before, even at my loneliest, at least I had my best friend, Ashley, nearby.

And now she isn't.

Or at least, she won't be when her parents take her away.

In the darkness, I stared at my computer screen and rubbed my face. I had been given a standard sleeping room somewhere in the depths of the military base. Two soldiers stood outside in the hallway to guard my room. It felt like I was in a prison cell again.

I kept seeing Ashley's stunned face and feeling the grip of her hand on mine. *What would it be like,* I asked myself again, *to meet parents you didn't remember?* When she'd left the room with them, she'd stared back at me with a sad and scared face. I couldn't get it out of my mind.

As a result, I hadn't been able to sleep, so I'd decided to add to my diaries. These had begun when the dome on Mars started to run out of oxygen. Mom had said it might be good for people on Earth to see life on Mars from a kid's point of view. Even though the dome had survived the crisis, I had continued with my diary entries. Although I'd never admit it to Mom, now I liked putting my thoughts on paper. It helped me sort them out.

And now, at least, focusing on what to put in the diary might take my mind off my loneliness.

I began to type on the keyboard, trying to put together all the things Cannon and I had talked about in some kind of order. The things I'd been thinking about a lot lately.

> Someone tried to kill me today. Not because of anything I've done, but because of a worldwide political divide that began before I was born. Because of water and food and energy shortages from massive population overgrowth, it became apparent that a nuclear war might break out and cause human extinction. Out of all the proposed solutions, two became popular enough for debate. One side said humans should seek to expand beyond Earth. The other side, which became known as the Terratakers, called for "drastic reduction of growth." They didn't want to waste valuable resources on space exploration.

I stopped. I felt like I was writing an essay as homework. But I knew it should be in my diary. Sometimes I daydreamed that my diaries would survive on DVD-gigarom for hundreds of years and that far, far into the future, a kid like me might stumble across them and begin to read.

Whenever I had that daydream, I realized how amazing reading and writing were. Without them, humans would not be able to pass on much information from one generation to the next. And reading what someone wrote was like hearing them speak in your mind, no matter how much time and distance had passed. So, in a way, I had the chance to talk to someone hundreds of years in the future. If they happened to find my diaries. . . .

So as I keyboarded, I began to imagine I was telling this directly to a kid living in another solar system. He or she might think this was so ancient, hearing about the squabbles on the tiny planet of Earth, billions of miles away. But if it was ancient history to him or her, it was also important. Because if the Terratakers succeeded in stopping space expansion, the chance to read it from another solar system would never happen.

The scariest part of the Terratakers' political philosophy was the phrase "drastic reduction of growth." They wanted governments across the world to run lotteries for licenses that allowed parents to have children. They wanted to be able to put to death undesirable people who were disabled, terminally ill, simply too old and unhealthy, or who tested positive for a genetic disease via their DNA. Which meant someone like me, in a wheelchair, might be seen as someone who should be eliminated to save oxygen and water.

Fortunately, as the issue was debated country by country, the voters rejected mandatory population control. It was too dangerous to allow government officials to play God by deciding who lived and who didn't. So the end result was to expand beyond Earth. This led to a whole new set of problems.

The goal of expansion was only possible if all the countries in the world joined together. But none wanted to lose independence. In the end, the former United Nations became the World United Federation. But it was not a one-world government with a common currency and one leader. The political structures in each country remained unchanged, and each country elected and sent one governor to the twice-yearly Summit of Governors. As part of this, every country in the world signed a 100-year treaty to pledge resources and technology to expansion on the Moon and Mars.

There was still opposition, however. It was costing billions and billions to support the Mars Project—billions and billions that tapped into Earth resources and made life more difficult for the growing Earth population. Which also meant higher taxes. Many within each country did not like making the sacrifice in this generation for the next. Because they had been unable to get their way in the political process, they turned to terrorism. They became part of the Terratakers.

Now, it appeared, I was included among their targets. Me and kids like me who controlled robots were the next step in space exploration. To stop expansion then, they had to stop us and—

Someone knocked on the door and I stopped keyboarding.

"Yes?" I called. I wasn't too worried. If the Terratakers had somehow made it into the depths of the Combat Force base and overcome the soldiers who guarded me, I doubt they would have knocked before entering my room. "Come in."

The door opened.

I hit save on my computer and spun in my wheelchair.

It was Ashley.

"Hey," I said.

"Hey yourself," she replied. "I didn't know if I'd have a chance to say good-bye in the morning."

"Not a big deal," I said. Even though it was.

"Yeah. Not a big deal," she repeated slowly. "I'll only be gone for a day or so. Cannon says he still needs me to help you on the Moon. After that . . ."

Something about the way she hesitated made me afraid.

"After that?"

"Well." She hesitated. "I mean, these are my parents. If I go to Mars to help assemble the carbon-dioxide generators, I might not see them for years and years. Cannon says it will be up to me whether to stay or go."

"I see," I said. And if she stayed, I would not see her for years and years.

"It's unfair," she returned. "Even if I wanted to go to Mars—and I think I do—how can I reject my parents? I'd feel guilty all my life. But they don't seem like my parents. I hardly know them."

"You've spent almost a day with them. How was it?"

She shrugged. "They seem like strangers. We get along, but it's hard to find things to talk about. I guess I shouldn't expect anything different, though."

I nodded. "At least you'll have the next few days."

"I'll miss you," she said softly.

"Yeah." I stared down at my lap. "I'll miss you too."

"Pardon? You mumbled something."

I coughed. "I'll miss you too."

"You'd better." She grinned. "But I have an idea. Remember the ant-bot?"

How could I not remember? It was a miniature robot. I didn't know its official name, but Ashley and I had always called it the *ant-bot*.

"In all the confusion when we got arrested after the trip from Mars, no one ever asked for it back. I've had it hidden with me the whole time."

That would have been easy enough. It was smaller than an ant, and on the outside it vaguely looked like one too.

"You want me to have it now?" I asked.

"No. I'm going to keep it with me. Tomorrow night, about this time, maybe you can visit. I mean, not you. But through the ant-bot."

"You got it," I said. I knew what she meant. "Tomorrow night."

She ran to me and kissed my forehead. Then she ran out of the room before I could say anything else.

In one way I felt good about that kiss on my forehead. And in another way, horrible. What if she decided not to return to Mars?

I shut my computer down. I couldn't sleep. But I sure didn't feel like writing any more diary stuff.

CHAPTER 10

A loud ring and a monotone voice woke me. I blinked until I was awake enough to realize it was the phone beside my bed, reporting that I had an incoming call. I groaned and reached for it. The alarm clock showed it was 5:00. As in 5:00 A.M. Hours before regular people woke. Unless there was a good reason for this call, I was going to be very grumpy with the person on the other end.

"Hello," I croaked.

"Tyce."

I knew this voice! Instantly I was wide awake. With no thoughts of being grumpy.

"Dad! Where are you? Are you all right?"

"You are mistaken. This is not your father. But I have a message for you."

"But—"

"Listen. When you have your upcoming interview, don't be afraid to tell her the truth. About anything and everything. Trust no one else."

Then silence.

"And?" I said. "Anything else you want to tell me?"

"Yes. Robots don't get headaches."

More silence. The person on the other end had hung up.

Slowly I placed the telephone back. I stared at the alarm clock and watched the red numbers change, minute by minute. But I wasn't really focused on the numbers. Not with the thoughts going through my head.

The man had said he wasn't my father. But I knew my father's voice. It couldn't have been anyone else. Plus only my father would have told me that robots don't get headaches. It was a private joke. Very private. Robots aren't supposed to get headaches, but their controllers sure get them. And I'd had plenty of them from the short circuits I'd gotten on several of our missions together. Had he said that so I would know it was him even though he had just denied it?

If that was true, what was going on? And what was this about an upcoming interview?

"Tyce," Cannon said to me a couple of hours later.

"Yes, sir?" I had just eaten breakfast. Not tasteless nutrient-tube food, like we got on Mars, but real scrambled eggs, bacon, and toast with fresh strawberry jam. We were in a cafeteria—except the general called it a *canteen*—that overlooked the Combat Force base's runway. I sat with my wheelchair directly facing the windows. I'd gone my whole life seeing that butterscotch sky and blue sun on Mars. I couldn't get enough of Earth's blue sky and yellow sun.

"So that Ashley will have all day today with her parents," Cannon continued, "the Moon shuttle is set for tomorrow afternoon. That will give her most of tomorrow with her parents too. In the meanwhile, I'll give you a briefing."

I watched a jet land. The wing flaps were extended. Its nose was tilted up slightly. When the wheels hit the runway, a puff of smoke briefly blossomed behind it. It was an incredible sight. No one in the canteen seemed to be paying attention.

"Briefing?" I'd seen ads on television about undergarments, but this . . .

He smiled, and his stern face relaxed. "Sorry. I keep speaking military around you. A briefing means an information session. We'll continue from what you already know. Essentially we've already dropped robots into place on the Moon. One for you and one for Ashley. The robots are hidden just outside the warehouse in the Manchurian Sector. You and Ashley will go into robot control from a ship in orbit around the Moon."

He grinned and shook his head. "You know, talking like this shows me how old I am. When I was your age, a Moon trip was incredibly expensive. Now it's like flying a commercial jet. We've got entire communities established under Moon domes. I mean, the last 20 years have been amazing in terms of space exploration."

I nodded. Someone had told me that there were people alive who'd been around before cell phones were invented. I could hardly believe that.

"My father," I said. I had decided to keep the early morning phone call to myself. "Any word on him?"

"Nothing. Yet. Everything possible is being done. He'll be found, I can assure you of that. In the meantime, we do have someone to make sure no Terratakers cause you any problems. On Earth or in orbit. He's your new escort."

He pointed over my shoulder.

I strained and turned to see a familiar face.

"Nate!"

He was wearing a grin that matched mine and his blue eyes sparkled.

"Good to see you, buddy," he said, rushing forward with his large hand ready to shake mine. "Scared up any gators lately?"

I'd first met Nate in the swamps of Florida, where he had almost been killed by an alligator. He, along with the general, had helped Ashley and me escape the Terratakers. His platoon buddies in the E.A.G.L.E.S., the elite division of the Combat Force of the World United Federation, had nicknamed him "Wild Man." When we met him, he had looked the part, with a big, bushy black beard and equally bushy long hair. Since then he had shaved and cut his hair. He'd swapped his tattered wilderness clothing for something fashionable and now looked very respectable. The things that gave his background away, however, were the bulging muscles of his chest and shoulders and arms. Not even clothing could hide that.

"Good to see you too," I said. I meant it. Crazy things had been happening, and having Nate around was like having an anchor in a storm.

"So," Nate said to the general, "what's first on our agenda?"

"Nothing much." Cannon smiled. "Just a committee hearing later this afternoon."

Nate made a gagging sound. "Committee hearing! I thought you didn't want to put Tyce's life in danger."

"Danger?" The general frowned.

"Danger. Committee hearings will bore anyone to the point of death."

"It should hold his interest," the general answered, with a twitch of a smile. "He'll be answering questions for a delegation from the ethics committee of the World United Federation. This robot control is as new to them as it is to the rest of the world."

Ethics committee? Was this the interview Dad meant? And if so, who was "she"?

The general turned to me. "Yesterday's news conference set off a chain reaction across the world. Politicians at all levels are getting concerned phone calls about the treatment of children who are 'attached' to robots. The ethics committee needs to hear from you in order to make some first-stage decisions on how to respond."

My face must have reflected my thoughts.

"Don't be nervous," the general commented. "They're on your side. They just want basic information about what it's like to control robots."

"Sure," I said doubtfully.

"And then there's an interview with Ms. Borris. You might remember her from the news conference."

An interview with Ms. Borris. Could this be the "she" Dad had predicted during that strange phone call a few hours earlier? If so, boy, did I have questions for her.

"It seems she wants to allow you to let the world know that it's not a bad thing to control robots. The interview will take an hour and—"

A soldier in a standard Combat Force jumpsuit rushed toward us. His hair was shaved close to his skull. Stopping a respectful distance away, he waited for the general to return his salute.

"Yes?" Cannon snapped off a quick salute.

"Sir, it's about the young Ashley and her family."

"Yes?" Cannon lost his relaxed air.

"First of all, I've been instructed to tell you that the DNA results were faked."

"Faked! Who did it? How?"

"I wasn't given that information, sir. But I can tell you why. You see, our surveillance team has lost them."

"Lost them! Impossible!"

"Sir, I've been told it did occur. I've also been told to relay this message to you. Sir, they think she's been kidnapped."

CHAPTER 11

An hour later, Nate began to blindfold me.

"Ready to find Ashley?" he asked. He was the only other person with me.

"Ready," I said, trying to calm myself. Questions raced through my mind. Where had she been taken? How? By whom? The Terratakers? What did they intend to do with her? Or was she even still alive? I didn't even want to consider that possibility.

"Headset next," Nate said.

"Right."

I was on a bed in a safe room somewhere deep in the Combat Force base. In a pinch, I could do this in my wheelchair, but the bed was more comfortable. Nate had already strapped me to the bed. With the blindfold came total darkness. Soon, when he finished pulling a headset down over my ears to block all sounds, the only sensory input to my brain would come from taste and touch and smell. But there wasn't much around to smell and taste, and since I couldn't move, my brain had already accustomed itself to the sensation of the straps that bound me in place.

All of this was important. I needed as few distractions

as possible, for I was about to enter robot control. My head was propped on a large pillow so that the plug at the bottom of my neck did not press on the bed. This plug had been spliced into my spine before I could walk so that the thousands of bioplastic microfibers could grow and intertwine with my nerve endings as my own body grew. Each microfiber's core transmitted tiny impulses of electricity through my spinal plug into another plug linked to a receiver. Then that receiver transmitted signals to the robot's computer drive. It worked just like the remote control of a television set, with two differences. Television remotes used infrared and were limited in distance. Just like with cell phones, this receiver was capable of trading information with a satellite that in turn bounced and received signals to and from anywhere in the world. And all at the speed of light, 186,000 miles per second. Since the world was only 25,000 miles around, it meant almost instant communication.

"Let me run a checklist past you," I said, facing upward in total blindness. It was something my friend Rawling had always done with me on Mars. He said it was very important, for the same reason that pilots run checklists before flying—safety. Nate didn't need the checklist; it was more a reminder for myself. More than that, it felt familiar. I needed that right now, when everything in my life seemed up for grabs.

"Fire away," Nate encouraged.

"No contact with any electrical sources. Ever." Any electrical current going into or through the robot would scramble the input so badly that the signals reaching my own nervous system could do serious damage to my brain.

"Check," Nate said.

"Second," I said, "disengage instantly at the first warning of any damage to the robot's computer drive." My brain circuits worked so closely with the computer circuits that any harm to the computer could spill over to harm my brain.

"Check."

"Final one," I said. "Robot battery at full power."

"Um . . ."

"I don't know either. But it's part of my checklist. Ashley's got the ant-bot. I can only assume since she intended for me to use it that she made sure it would be ready."

"This ant-bot," Nate began. "You're not making this up. Right?"

In the darkness beneath my blindfold, I laughed. "Not making it up. If a person can control a full-size robot, why not a miniature one?"

That was one of the many exciting possibilities for robot control. No computer ever built could rival the human brain. Through robot control, the brain gave commands to machines. Big robots. Microscopic robots. I'd once controlled a space torpedo. There was no reason robot control couldn't be extended to aircraft or submarines. The computer fired signals to a satellite, which bounced them back to the robot. In other words, I could stay on the bed in the military base and handle equipment anywhere in the world.

"Robot control," Nate said. "Ant-bot. All of this really messes with my mind. You know, when I was a kid, virtual reality was still a primitive type of game."

"Yeah," I said, grinning from my bed, "but that was ages ago . . . back when people listened to groups like 'N Sync or the Backstreet Boys. Now they might be in an old folks' home somewhere. So just remember. You *are* ancient."

"Ancient, maybe. But much bigger than you. And trained in the use of deadly force. Don't forget that."

"Also sworn to protect me, not threaten me," I answered.

"After I put on the headset, can I tape your mouth shut too?"

I was glad for the joking around. It took away some of my fear about Ashley. But I couldn't escape one question. What if her kidnappers had found the ant-bot and I couldn't communicate with her?

The answer to that would arrive in the next few minutes.

"I'm ready for the headset," I told Nate.

I felt him gently place the headset over my ears. Now I was completely trapped in darkness and silence. Which meant my brain would only respond to the signals from the robot.

I waited for the sensation of entering robot control. A feeling like I was falling off a cliff into a pitch-black void with no bottom.

It came.

Blind and in silence, I fell and fell and fell . . .

CHAPTER 12

Somewhere, on the other end of the satellite, signals bounced back and forth between my brain and the ant-bot's computer. I expected to "wake up" and see through the eyes of the ant-bot.

You see, with robot control, the information is simply sent to my brain from the robot's eyes and robot's ears. In turn, my brain sends the robot information on how to move, the same way the brain directs my human body when I'm disconnected from robot control. I see and hear what the robot sees and hears. It moves the way my brain directs. Temporarily, it's like my brain is inside the robot computer. All I have to do is mentally shout "Stop!" and I disengage my brain from robot control.

Strapped to the bed, I waited for the falling sensation to end and for light signals from the ant-bot to reach my brain.

But the blackness remained.

It was as dark to my brain as if I were seeing through my own blindfolded eyes. In fact, for a moment I wondered if I had even managed to successfully link a signal between my brain and the ant-bot. Perhaps Ashley wouldn't even check the ant-bot until the time we'd talked about—late tonight.

So I tested it by flexing my arms. I half expected to feel the pressure of straps against my skin. Instead I heard a tiny click, as if the robot's tiny titanium arms and hands had hit something metallic.

Which meant the link had been established. My brain *was* receiving signals from the ant-bot. That meant I needed to explore the world around the ant-bot.

Groping in the darkness, I felt around with the robot's hands. I slid backward. That was my own action. But I also felt the entire body of the ant-bot bounce up and down gently. This was happening *to* the ant-bot, not because of it.

So I was inside something that was being carried by someone. Hopefully that someone was Ashley.

My brain gradually adjusted to the signals reaching it, just like my own eyes adjusted to light. And far away I saw the tiniest crack of light.

I tried to reach it and was surprised to find it closer than I expected. I bumped into something like a tube.

Finally I realized.

It wasn't a tube but a hinge. With light coming through the tiniest of openings provided by the not-quite-perfect fit of the hinge.

I was inside Ashley's locket. The one her "parents" had given to her when they'd come to pick her up from the Combat Force base. The one they said they'd given her as a baby, kept all these years they thought she was dead, and now were finally able to give back to her.

I assumed she was wearing the locket around her neck. Rumblings vibrated through it and my ant-bot body.

Sound!

Loud sound!

Mentally I adjusted the sensitivity of the ant-bot's audio input.

The ant-bot works like a regular full-size robot, except on a smaller scale. The video lenses zoom from telescopic to microscopic. It can amplify hearing and pick up sounds at higher and lower levels than human hearing.

As I lowered the volume, the rumbling stopped, and the words began to make sense.

"Can you untie my hands so I can go to the bathroom?" This was Ashley's voice.

"Bathroom. Again?" said an annoyed voice.

I immediately guessed she'd been trying to get away from them often to open the locket and see if I was operating the ant-bot yet. This time I'd be there.

"I drank a lot of water. And like I keep telling you, it's not like I can jump out the window. Airplane bathrooms don't have windows. And you don't see me wearing a parachute."

They were flying.

Not good news. Every hour meant she could be another 500 or 600 miles farther away. In any direction.

There was good news, however. Back on the Combat Force base, computer experts were attempting to locate the ant-bot by tracking its satellite signal to the computer receiver on base. They needed three different satellites to link up and triangulate in order to locate the ant-bot's latitude and longitude and altitude. Because this triangulation wasn't instant, I needed to stay connected to the ant-bot.

"Don't bother arguing with her," another deeper voice said. "What's the big deal?"

"I don't trust her," the first voice answered. "Someone in her position should be more afraid. It's like she knows something we don't."

"We're untouchable," the second voice said. "No one is going to find us. Relax. Untie her hands."

I felt more movement as Ashley rose from her seat. At

least that was my guess. Stuck inside her locket, I didn't have much to go on.

A minute later light hit me, so bright that I nearly fell backward.

"Tyce?"

Ashley's gigantic face blocked much of the light. Her nose looked like a mountain to me.

"Ashley!" I shouted as loud as the ant-bot would permit. Once she'd visited me with the ant-bot. She'd crawled close to my ear and spoken in the middle of the night. This was before I knew the ant-bot existed, and I'd wondered if God was speaking out loud to me. Ashley had enjoyed scaring me with a voice from out of nowhere.

"Tyce?" She lifted the locket toward her ear.

"Ashley!" My voice sounded very tiny and tinny. I hoped she could hear me above the airplane noise. "Ashley!"

"Finally," she said. "I've tried a dozen times!"

She held the locket so close to her ear that I could have reached up and grabbed one of her hairs. Only to me, controlling the ant-bot, it would have been like grabbing a thick, thick rope.

"They weren't my parents," she said. "They were actors."

"I know," I answered. "And I found out the doctor who supplied the false DNA test has disappeared. This was a well-planned kidnapping."

"Well planned is right," she added. "And planned right inside the military by World United Federation Combat Force soldiers. I'm on one of their jets right now. The sun is coming through the right-hand windows."

World United Federation Combat Force soldiers. So there *were* even more traitors in the military than I'd thought. And that meant . . .

"Good-bye!" I shouted into Ashley's ear. There was no time to explain.

In my mind, I gave the "Stop!" command.

And just like that, I ended robot control.

Leaving Ashley all alone on an airplane headed away from safety at hundreds of miles per hour.

CHAPTER 13

Fifteen minutes later I faced Cannon and Nate. Outside. Near the runway of the Combat Force base. With jets taking off and their engines howling.

"What is going on?" Cannon said loudly. "I thought you said you could find Ashley with that miniature robot."

His last words ended with a shout, as he tried to make himself heard above the jet engines.

I pointed at the jet.

"She's in one like that!" I shouted back. "And I needed to talk to you about it where no one could overhear us with electronic bugging devices."

"What!" Wind whipped at my hair and the general's clothes. Nate, like a solid rock, seemed untouched.

"I said I want to make sure no one can hear us!"

"I can't hear you!"

"Exactly!"

"What!" he shouted.

Finally the jet left the runway. Seconds later the noise began to recede.

"I wanted to be at a place where no one could overhear us with electronic surveillance equipment. Ashley says she was kidnapped by Combat Force soldiers."

"You made contact!" This from the general. Nate had no expression. He just stood motionless, listening to our conversation.

"She's in a military jet." I told them what had happened.

"And you immediately left her—" Cannon frowned as he hesitated and thought it through—"because if someone in the Combat Force had taken her, that means someone high up must have ordered the operation. And that higher-up is working for the Terratakers. So if the triangulation was successful, and we learned Ashley's location and sent in soldiers to rescue her, then word of that would have reached the traitor, and he would be in a position to have his soldiers search for the ant-bot and move Ashley again before our soldiers arrived."

"Exactly," I said.

The general's frown deepened. "That fits. The fake reports are easy to deliver if someone on the inside wanted it that way. And the only way our surveillance could have lost her is if they let it happen. That's the trouble with a military organization with hundreds of thousands of soldiers who come from hundreds of different countries across the world. The strength of the structure is diversity. But that also leads to its weakness. More difficult to control. There are 60 generals of my rank. Any one of them could have his own power base to run a secret military operation. So all it takes is one general to believe in the Terrataker cause for something like this to happen."

"What next?" I asked.

"You're going to have to find her without the triangulation," Cannon said. "Which means we need to hope and pray that she stays alive long enough to tell you."

"Why?" I asked.

"Why hope and pray?" Cannon gave me a strange look. He knew what I believed about God.

"Sorry. I meant why kidnap her. She's just one of the robot controllers. There are all the other pods full of control kids. But they took only her."

"I wish I could answer that," Cannon said. "But at least all the others are safe. Can you imagine if the Manchurians got the Terratakers to regain control of them too?"

"In the meantime," Nate put in, "we've got to keep Tyce safe. If we can't trust our own people, who's to say he won't be kidnapped next?"

"Impossible." But Cannon's tone told us he didn't really believe it to be impossible.

"Sir, a faked doctor report and dropped surveillance. I think there's enough of a hidden organization within the Combat Force to make anything happen."

"You're right." Cannon sighed. "But it's absolutely crucial that Tyce faces the ethics committee this afternoon. And does the interview with Ms. Borris this evening. But now that Ashley's been kidnapped and we don't know what the Terratakers are up to, it's important for Tyce to handle the robot on the Moon today to help us find those kids as soon as possible. Any suggestions on how to do all of those things within a short time frame, Nate?"

"I have an idea," I said.

Both of them looked at me.

"How long would it take to get me into space?"

CHAPTER 14

This is what it would be like to walk on the Moon, I thought, in awe four hours later as my robot rolled forward on the Moon's dusty-looking surface.

The first thing I noticed was the sky. Mars, where I was born, has some atmosphere. The Moon has none. Because of it, the sky was jet-black. It seemed like a blanket I could reach up and pull around me, with tiny white holes burned through the blanket by starlight.

And it was very quiet. With no air to transmit sounds, my robot's audio didn't even pick up the slight squeaks that usually happened as the titanium arms moved back and forth. There was no soft squishing sound as the robot wheels sank into the soil.

But it wasn't really soil. And, at extremely low gravity, the robot didn't sink far.

The surface of the Moon isn't like loose dirt you might walk through in bare feet on Earth. It's like gray baby powder, a talcum of the softest dust you might ever run through your fingers.

However, a half inch below the surface it felt like cement. Without air molecules to separate the dust molecules, the weight of my robot on the narrow wheels—even with the lower gravity—was enough to compact the dust. It would be the same for you walking on the Moon. You would sink that half inch in the powder and leave behind perfect footprints that would forever remain preserved, with the sharp edges of your tread never blurred by wind or water.

What I loved the most about moving across the surface of the Moon were the patterns of dust from my spinning wheels. With no air and no wind to affect it, the kicked-up powder slowly, slowly fell in perfect semicircles away from my wheels.

I could have rolled forward for miles and miles, enjoying the peace around me.

But I had a job to do.

Ahead was the low flat building that I had seen on the slide show in the Combat Force jet with General Cannon. Parked outside, just like the photos I'd seen, were platform buggies that moved supplies in and out of the building.

I had my instructions. Get the robot body beneath a platform buggy. Secure it in place on an axle. And wait until the platform buggy brought the robot body inside.

Which I did. Successfully. Ten minutes later, my robot was hidden beneath the platform buggy.

But that was only the beginning.

When I finished, I called "Stop!" and all the sights and sounds and sensations delivered to me by the robot's video and audio outputs faded away. An instant later I saw the darkness of the blindfold over my own eyes and heard the silence of the headset in my own ears.

Because in that instant, my mind had traveled 125,000 miles from the Moon to where I was currently. Hung in a small space station in orbit halfway between the Moon and New York City.

And while I wouldn't be leaving the space station for the next while, I'd be visiting a lot of different places with different robots.

CHAPTER 15

Ten minutes later—with just enough time on the small space station to say hello to Nate and go for a bathroom and water break—and another 125,000 miles below, I began to speak through a second robot body in New York City to the ethics committee of the World United Federation.

Seven Vice-Governors sat behind a long narrow table, each with a brass-engraved nameplate resting directly in front. Beside each nameplate was a comp-board.

All of the men looked as gray as the surface of the Moon. And just as old. They appeared so similar that it was hard for me to distinguish between them. They all wore gray suits and had gray hair and gray beards. And their expressions were gray—no smiles, no frowns. Just wrinkles that seemed carved into their gray skin.

They stared at my robot, so it felt like they were staring at me.

My robot faced the long, narrow table.

"How much longer do we have to wait for the robot to start talking?" one hoarse voice said. This came from a man who sat behind the nameplate marked *Vice-Governor Patterson*.

"Frankly," another Vice-Governor named Calvin answered in an equally worn-out voice, "I think this is all hogwash."

Hogwash? These men washed hogs? They were Vice-Governors, which was the position just below Supreme Governor. From the world's 200 Vice-Governors, the Supreme Governor was elected every four years. If the other 193 were like these stuffy-looking old men, the world was in big trouble.

"I agree," Vice-Governor Armitage said. "It's nonsense. Probably some Hollywood stunt to promote a new movie. Trying to tell us the boy is in orbit and will hook up to this robot anytime now."

Oh, I realized, hogwash was nonsense. Earth expressions were weird.

"If he does start talking, I'm going to have a difficult time believing it's him," Vice-Governor Armitage said. "It looks like a praying mantis."

I knew I should speak to let them know I'd arrived, but I was curious to know which way this meeting might go. Vice-Governor Armitage's comment didn't surprise me or hurt my feelings. The robot's upper body did look like a praying mantis. It was sticklike, with a short, thick, hollow pole that stuck upward from an axle at the bottom that connected two wheels. At the upper end of the pole was a head and a crosspiece, to which the arms were attached. Four video lenses served as eyes, and three tiny microphones, attached to the underside of the video lens, played the role of ears, taking in sound. A speaker, on the underside of the video lens that faced forward, produced sound and allowed me to make my voice heard.

The computer drive of the robot was well protected within the hollow titanium pole that served as the robot's upper body. A short antenna plug-in at the back of the pole took signals to and from my brain.

Another Vice-Governor—*Michaels*, from what it said on his nameplate—moved out from behind the table and shuffled toward the robot. He peered directly into my video lens. I could see the veins in his yellowing eyeballs.

The old man tapped the robot's forward video lens.

"Ouch," I said.

Vice-Governor Michaels jumped backward, nearly falling.

Instantly the murmuring at the table stopped. Vice-Governor Michaels inched away until he reached the table, as if he were afraid I would attack him.

"Hello," I said through the robot's audio. "I am Tyce Sanders. I am controlling this robot. General Jeb McNamee said you might be interested in speaking with me."

"We want to speak with Tyce Sanders," Vice-Governor Armitage said. "Not a robot."

"I wish I could," I answered. "But—"

"Yes," Vice-Governor Armitage said with an impatient wave. "General McNamee explained this situation. Something about the speed of light and trying to have you in two places at the same time. Still, the ethics committee is not to be trifled with."

"Yes, sir," I said. "It is necessary that I also control a robot on the Moon. It is a quarter million miles from the Earth to the Moon. So if I were on Earth, the signals would have to travel to the Moon and back. That would mean too much of a time lag, because even at the speed of light that half million miles takes a little over a second. Ideally, I should be orbiting the Moon so the signal would be almost instant. As it was, we settled on a halfway point. From that place in orbit, I can control robots on Earth. And also, later, on the Moon."

I didn't add that being on a small space station was also the safest spot possible. Terratakers would not be able to reach me. One hundred and twenty-five thousand miles of outer space served much better than any moat around any castle. At least that was the way Nate had put it.

"Anyway," I finished, "there is a slight lag between sending a signal and the robot reacting, but it is workable."

"Sending a signal." Vice-Governor Calvin peered at me with some suspicion. "Am I to understand this robot responds to your brain commands?"

"It was in the report," Vice-Governor Patterson snapped. "Must you always waste our time like this?"

"I want to hear it directly from the boy." Vice-Governor Calvin didn't seem disturbed in the least by Vice-Governor Patterson's outburst. He must have been used to it.

I explained. All of it. With plenty of stops for more questions and interruptions. An hour later all of them finally understood the concept. The delays were driving me crazy. All I could think about was Ashley and how I needed to get my committee, interview, and Moon mission over and get back to finding her as soon as possible. This wasn't like juggling balls, something I'd taught myself to do on Mars. I mean, drop a ball and no big deal. But could I live with myself if I made a mistake with what I was juggling now?

"Please," Vice-Governor Patterson said with a sigh, "may we get to the important ethical questions?"

"Certainly," Vice-Governor Calvin said calmly. "We're not here to waste time."

"Ahem." Vice-Governor Michaels faked a cough. "Explain to us how it was that you asked for this operation that allowed bioplastic fibers to grow into your nervous system. I understand you were just starting to walk at the time."

"Yes, sir," my robot said to Vice-Governor Michaels. "But I did not ask for the operation."

Vice-Governor Michaels made a note on his compboard.

"Who authorized the operation?" Vice-Governor Patterson asked.

"I believe it was the World United Federation, sir. The operation was very expensive, but it did get full approval."

"Let me rephrase," Patterson said. "Who allowed you to be operated on?"

"My mother," I said.

"So you had no choice in the matter."

"No, sir. But if they had waited until I was old enough to make the choice, I would have been too old for the operation. It has to be done at a very young age to allow the nervous system and bioplastic fibers to grow together properly."

"In other words," Vice-Governor Michaels said to Vice-Governor Patterson, "we have over 200 children who all had the operation done without their consent. And if we want to take advantage of this new technology, we will have to continue operating on children who have no choice. The world may be a better place with this new technology, but they'll pay the price."

"Sir," I said. All eyes turned to the robot.

I continued. "Since I have been this way all of my life—at least as far back as I can remember—I have never thought of it as paying a price. Being able to explore outer space and Mars through the body of a robot has been something so great I can hardly describe it—"

"Really," Vice-Governor Michaels said, cutting me off.

His eyes turned flinty. "Because of the operation, you've spent your whole life in a wheelchair. You might know what it is like to walk on Mars or on the Moon, but you don't know what it's like to walk on Earth. So let me ask you this. If I could guarantee an operation that would allow you to walk but take away your ability to control robots, would you have it done?"

"That is an unfair question," I said, stunned. "I was the only one out of all the kids who suffered spinal-cord damage because of the operation."

"In the future, mistakes will happen again. Would you trade your robot control to be fully human?"

"Are you suggesting that because I need a wheelchair, I am not fully human?" I insisted as hotly as I could through my robot voice.

Vice-Governor Michaels blushed. "Let me rephrase that. Would you trade your robot control to be able to walk? Would you allow us to operate on another child, knowing that this child, too, might suffer the same nerve damage you did?"

I couldn't answer. That would be like playing God with someone else's life.

After long seconds, Vice-Governor Michaels sat back in his chair. "As I thought," he said. "I don't think we need to ask any further questions."

CHAPTER 16

Half an hour later my robot rolled in the low gravity and zero atmosphere of the Moon. In orbit, where my body was hooked to computers, I wasn't tired yet. I'd just been in New York through one robot body, and now I was back on the Moon through another.

Here, in the Moon dust, my robot couldn't show emotion, of course, but my own excitement was nearly enough that it bounced forward.

The plan had succeeded!

During my time with the ethics committee in New York, someone here on the Moon had moved the platform buggy inside the low flat building above the mining operation.

That meant they had also moved my robot inside. When I had entered robot control, my robot was already past whatever security system there was guarding this warehouse. Amid all the activity inside, no one had noticed as I'd lowered the robot onto the ground and out from beneath the buggy.

There were probably two dozen men working in space suits. I assumed they came in daily from the closest sector of the

Moon dome—the Manchurian Sector. The men were working at various tasks, but most were moving pallets of boxes from one end of the building to the other.

Then one man noticed my robot. He gestured at it from beneath his helmet, then moved it into an elevator. A short ride took me down. When the doors opened, I was in a gigantic vault. And ahead, I saw about 20 robots like the one I operated. They held equipment that looked like giant torches and were cutting out blocks of material. It was obvious that their work had expanded this giant vault to the size it was. I couldn't imagine how many months they had already been doing this.

It only took a couple of seconds to move beside the nearest robot.

"Hello," I said. "We need to talk."

The robot kept pointing the giant welding torch into the rock face.

"Hello!" I shouted. "We need to talk!"

Still it ignored me.

Then I remembered.

We were on the Moon. No air. Which meant no sound waves.

They couldn't hear me. I couldn't hear them. Was this rescue attempt over before it could begin?

"Nate!"

Almost immediately he removed my blindfold and headset.

"Back from the Moon already?" he asked. He unstrapped my arms and legs. I sat up and rubbed my wrists.

"I'm back," I said. The familiar walls of the small space

station loomed above me. Or below me. Or beside me. It was hard to guess. In space, there's no up or down or sideways.

"What did you find out?" Nate asked.

"We couldn't talk." I grinned. "But we could scratch in the Moon dirt."

It had taken a while, but I'd finally learned from one robot what I needed.

The kids weren't staying on the Moon. They were on a space station somewhere. In orbit around the Moon. The rest I could guess. It was just like the pod of kids we discovered in Parker, Arizona, where Ashley was before she came to Mars. They were hooked up on permanent life support, unable to move out of their jelly tubes, living only through their robots.

"So," I said, after I explained that to Nate, "let's go rescue them."

"Sounds good to me. I'll call Cannon and tell him what we found out."

"Just one little thing," I said. "Down on Earth where I'm headed next. That dumb interview with Ms. Borris."

CHAPTER 17

That evening, through the video lens of my robot, I stared directly into a television camera. Behind the camera was the operator, a skinny man with a ponytail who had only been introduced to me as Ben.

The robot was in a television studio. The backdrop behind it was of New York City at night. In front of my robot was a coffee table with magazines. In a chair beside the robot was the legendary Ms. Borris. She wore black again, and I overheard her joking to the cameraman that it was her favorite color because it helped her look slim. Her natural hair was curly and cropped short. It looked far better than the platinum wig had when she pretended to be a nurse.

I thought of the mysterious phone call. How I believed it had been my father telling me I could trust Ms. Borris. And how, if it *had* been my father, he knew the interview would be taking place.

"Remember," Ms. Borris told me, interrupting my thoughts, "normally this is taped. But there has been such a demand for this exclusive interview that we are going live tonight to our worldwide audience."

"How's my hair?" I asked. With my robot arms, I pretended to smooth out imaginary hair on the robot's head.

Ms. Borris smiled. It took away much of her fierceness. "Nice touch," she said. "I wish the camera had been rolling when you did that. It would be a great opening shot to this news documentary."

Live to a worldwide audience. I reminded myself to be careful of what I did and said through the robot.

"Ready?" she asked.

"I have a bunch of questions for you." I lowered the robot's voice. "When are we going to be able to talk about—"

"Camera's rolling," Ben said. "Live in five . . . four . . ."

"Ready," I said. Cannon had insisted that favorable and immediate television exposure was probably more important to the future of robot control than the recommendations of the ethics committee of the World United Federation. If people saw that robots were nothing to be afraid of and if they saw good use for robot control, their mass opinion would force Vice-Governors all across the world to allow more tax money to be spent on robotics. The only trouble was the questions in the back of my mind I couldn't escape.

Would I trade my robot control to be able to walk again? Would I allow an operation on another child, knowing that this child, too, might suffer the same nerve damage I had?

I sure hoped Ms. Borris wouldn't ask those questions.

"Three . . ." Ben continued to count down.

Ms. Borris calmly sipped from a glass of water and set it down.

"Two . . . and—"

Ms. Borris spoke directly at the camera, reading from

the TelePrompTer that scrolled words on a screen in front of her.

"I'd like to introduce to you Tyce Sanders. Well, not Tyce himself, but a robot that he controls. Later in our show, we'll give you some of the technical details that make it possible for a human to control robots. You may, however, already know some of this. As I'm sure you're aware, very recently it was the robot Tyce controlled that prevented a nuclear meltdown just outside of Los Angeles."

Ms. Borris turned to me. "First of all," she said, "let's talk about the situation you're in right now. It will give our viewers a sense of the potential of robot control. As I understand it, because of threats upon your life, you currently control this robot from a space station that's in orbit between the Moon and Earth."

"Yes," I said. I explained that in the afternoon I had answered questions via robot for the ethics committee. I didn't tell her, of course, about my brief time on the Moon and what I had learned there.

"Let's get back to the ethics committee later," she said. "I'm fascinated by the fact that you can almost be in two places at once. Are you telling me that if you had access to 20 robots all across the world, you could go from one to another to another?"

"Yes," I said. "I cannot switch instantly, but it is possible."

"So you could speak to me here in New York and five minutes later speak to someone else in London, England? And then five minutes later, Paris? And so on?"

"If a robot was waiting in each place." I thought of the ant-bot in Ashley's locket. And wanted this interview to be over so I could try to talk to Ashley again.

"Is it tiring?"

"Physically, it is not." I explained how, during robot control, I was totally motionless. "Mentally, I can last as long as I would normally be able to stay awake and concentrate."

And so our conversation continued. I answered questions about growing up on Mars. I told her how it felt to go into robot control and how it felt to come out again. I told her about the capabilities of robots. That took well over a half hour of interview time.

After a short break, she continued with her questions. By then I was totally relaxed.

"You were able to go into a nuclear plant under extreme conditions," she began.

"Actually, my robot was. I directed its actions."

"Of course." She smiled. "Tell me, Tyce, if a robot is that unstoppable, wouldn't it make the perfect soldier?"

"It makes the perfect firefighter. It makes the perfect worker in extreme weather conditions. It makes the perfect explorer on the Moon and on Mars," I explained.

"But . . ." She leaned in. A fierceness filled her face. "If there were 200 of you orbiting in space and all 200 of you controlled armed robots down here on Earth, wouldn't you be perfect soldiers? Don't you see potential danger in that?"

"Who would build the 200 armed robots?" I asked. "Who would put them in place?"

My question seemed to catch her off guard. "I suppose," she answered, "it would be military people."

"Then," I said, "maybe you should ask them those questions."

For a moment, she frowned. Then she laughed. "Good point. Let's get to the operation itself. I understand it must be done before children are three years old. With adults, for example, the nervous system is too fully developed and won't properly intertwine with the bioplastic fibers that deliver information to the brain."

"That is correct," I answered. Now it was coming.

"So this operation is done to children before they are old enough to decide if they want it done or not."

"Yes." What was I going to say if she asked me if I would have allowed it to be done to me?

"So what if kids were taken from their parents at a young age and put into robot slavery?"

This wasn't the question I expected. I hesitated too long.

"What if," she continued, "I told you information has reached me that exactly this has *already* been done?"

"Then I would say that anyone who has that information and is holding it back to get better ratings on a show instead of helping those kids is using them just as badly as the people who put them into slavery," I fired back.

I expected her to get angry.

Instead, she smiled. "You are exactly right, Tyce Sanders. And that is why, right now, to a live worldwide audience, our network is going to break an exclusive story on how kids forced into slavery and armed with soldier robots almost assassinated all the officials at the recent Summit of Governors."

On a nearby television screen, I saw that the show cut from our interview and began to roll with the news story.

"How do you know all this?" I asked Ms. Borris through my robot. We were now off camera. Her exclusive story was giving out top secret military information.

"I'll tell you everything," she said. The bright, sharp expression on her face had been replaced by one of deep weariness. "Later tonight. If I'm not arrested by then."

"But—"

"Ten o'clock tonight. Make sure you return to controlling this robot. I'll have it all arranged so we can talk."

"Tonight?" There was Ashley. And the Moon stuff. "But—"

"Tonight," she insisted. "Your father's life depends on it."

CHAPTER 18

I had to remind myself that my body was remaining in one place, the nice quiet calm of outer space. Because everything else seemed like a whirlwind. The Moon. Then the ethics committee in New York. The Moon again. Back to New York for Ms. Borris. It was as hectic as playing a computer game full-time.

And now?

The visuals from the ant-bot brought a weird mixture of light and dark to my brain. At first, I had trouble focusing. It took some zooming out with the ant-bot lenses until I began to comprehend that I was not in Ashley's locket. It seemed like the ant-bot was screened from the light by something.

Hair?

"Ashley? Ashley?"

Without warning, brightness overwhelmed the ant-bot. It seemed like it was at the bottom of a tunnel.

"Hang on, Tyce."

Ashley! Talking to me in a whisper.

"I'm going to tilt my head and hold my hand below my ear," she continued to whisper. "Then crawl out onto my palm."

So it *had* been hair from her head that had screened the ant-bot from the light.

And she had hidden me in her ear?! Gross.

My entire world shifted, and I struggled to keep the ant-bot balanced.

"Ready," she said.

So I crawled out of her ear and onto her palm.

She held her hand up in front of her face. I peered upward through the video lenses of the ant-bot. To me, her face seemed as big as the presidents' faces carved into Mount Rushmore. I'd read about them once on an Earth history DVD-gigarom.

"I'm glad you're back," she said. "Why did you leave?"

I explained.

"That makes total sense. And it's probably the best thing you could have done. They took me to the one place no one would ever look for me. And I think our only chance is if they don't know you guys know."

"I don't have much time," I told her quickly. Ten o'clock, New York time, was approaching. I had to make sure I was in the robot in the television studio to talk with Ms. Borris. "It would be nice if you started making sense."

"Tyce," she said, sounding tired, "I'm back with all the other robot-control kids. In the mountains of Arizona."

"So you're safe then."

"No."

"No?"

"I remember a story once," Ashley whispered, as if she was afraid of being overheard. "It was about a woman who was so scared of being robbed that she put bars on all her windows and a dozen locks on her door. Her house caught on fire, and she couldn't get out."

"Meaning?" I asked. I was conscious of how little time I had. "Help me out with your riddle."

"Meaning," she answered softly, "the perfect place of protection can also be the perfect trap. The Combat Force soldiers are in control of a fortress no one can get into. But no one can get out of it either. The only link is by telephone or computer. Combat Force soldiers at other bases have no way of knowing anything is wrong here if someone on this end of the communications system lies to them."

I had a horrible feeling. My earlier conversation with Cannon came back to me. The one where I'd asked why Ashley had been kidnapped if there were all the others.

And Cannon's words echoed through my mind: *But at least all the others are safe. Can you imagine if the Manchurians got the Terratakers to regain control of them too?*

"What you're saying—" I gulped—"is that the wrong Combat Force people control this. And you're all prisoners."

She nodded. "The Terratakers have us again. They'll blow this place to shreds if anyone tries to take it. With us in it."

CHAPTER 19

When I left the ant-bot and began controlling the robot in New York City at ten o'clock, Ms. Borris was not waiting for me as promised.

Instead, when light waves reached my brain through the video lenses of the robot that had been left behind in the television studio, I found the robot alone in a small room. In front of a television.

I tried the door.

It was locked by a keyed bolt. No one could enter without the key. No one could leave without the key. The door was a steel fire door. I doubted even a robot could break through. What kind of trick did she think she was playing? I wondered. Trapping the robot wasn't like trapping me. All I had to do was disengage anytime I wanted.

Did she expect me to wait?

Or, it hit me, had she been taken somewhere so she couldn't be back on time? Had she been arrested, like she feared?

I looked again at the television and the remote sitting on top.

I wheeled over, took the remote, then backed away from

the television. When I pressed the remote, the screen flickered immediately to life. Ms. Borris stared straight at my robot from the screen. There was no backdrop behind her. Just a close-up of her face, looking fatigued.

"Tyce," her television figure said, "earlier today I locked your robot into this closet for fear that right after our interview, I would be arrested by the Combat Force for the subjects we discussed on television. *Kidnapped* is a better word, because I have done nothing to deserve being arrested. I knew the questions I was asking you would get me into trouble. I prerecorded this in case that happened. If I am not speaking to you in person, then you know I am in trouble. The only way to safety for all of us is for you to bring the whole truth about robot control to the world by media limelight. Not even the Terrataker traitors within the World United Federation can fight massive public opinion. Thank God, democracy still rules."

She paused to lift a glass of water into sight. She sipped from the glass, then set it down out of sight again. "Let me start by telling you that your father is not who he appears to be. For years, as a space pilot, he has been working undercover for the United States division of the Combat Force. As have I. We are both dedicated to stopping the Terratakers, and all of those aligned with the Manchurians who back them, from reaching world dominance within the Federation."

Dad? *My* dad? If robots could breathe, I'm sure mine would have held its breath as I kept watching through its eyes.

"General McNamee arranged for your father to escape the Combat Force prison in the Florida Everglades while you were in Arizona. In so doing, McNamee risked his career. There are higher-ranking generals within the World United

Federation who *do* serve the Terratakers. If they found out he was responsible . . ."

She took a deep breath. "You do know they are holding his son as a hostage."

Where was she going with this? And how did she know?

"The general is playing a complicated game," she continued, her video image looking directly ahead into the camera. "The higher-ups put him in charge of the robot-control technology because they have his son as a hostage and know they can control him. They tied the general's hands by telling him next to nothing about the operation. This way it would look like officially they have done their best. Unofficially, they could try to stop him. Yet, because of you and Ashley, he was able to prevent the assassination attempt at the Summit of Governors. They do not intend to let him go any farther. He can't openly fight the Terratakers hidden within the ranks above him or they might kill his son. Nor can he openly divulge military secrets to the media as a result of the Combat Force oath he took."

Where had she gotten all of this information?

"That is why he arranged for your father's escape. Your father has been feeding me the information it will take to defeat the Terratakers through media publicity. Cannon can't speak directly, so he has funneled information to your father."

She knew where Dad was!

"You may also be aware of the highly sophisticated electronic listening devices available to the Combat Force. It wouldn't surprise me if one was attached directly to your clothing. Or your wheelchair. Anywhere that will let some of the Terratakers listen to any of your conversations. For that reason, the general has been able to say little to you. And for that reason, your father has not been able to contact you directly, except for that one phone call."

She took another sip of water. "He was hoping you would be able to visit him in a robot body, which wouldn't be bugged. But he was also afraid that something might happen to me or that somehow we might get caught together, so he has only contacted me via telephone or computer. I don't know where he is. I can only tell you what he told me. And that he is safe."

Ms. Borris closed her eyes briefly. She looked sad and tired. I think I understood why. She expected to be arrested any minute. That made it all the more brave that she had decided to videotape this message instead of fleeing to somewhere safe.

"You'll find your father at the place that he and Rawling hung out in New York during their training days."

Rawling? They knew each other before the Mars Project? What kind of training had they done together?

My mind spun with possibilities.

"Your father says that Rawling won't give out that information unless he knows it's you asking. So even if the wrong people listen to this message, they won't be able to find him. But you can. Let me repeat. At the place that he and Rawling hung out in New York."

She sighed. "With me gone, you're the link, Tyce. You need to get all of this story broadcast to the world. Then your dad can come out of hiding. And I will be released. If I'm still alive."

There was noise behind her. She whirled her head in the direction of the noise. Then back at the camera. She began to talk very quickly. "I trust Ben, my cameraman. He's promised to lock your robot in a closet with this video ready to play. I hear the soldiers coming now. Get the information from Rawling. Find your father. He's got a way to reach the world media. Understand? Get to your father."

But the door was locked.

She smiled on camera, as if reading my mind. "You'll find a key taped beneath the television set. It will let you out of the closet. From there, get out of the building through a fire exit as fast as you can. And please, find your father!"

The television went dark.

CHAPTER 20

"Nate?" It was my voice speaking, not a robot's voice. I wasn't seeing through a robot's video lenses in New York or in Arizona or on the Moon. I was seeing through my eyes, the ones that had been blindfolded to make my robot control easier.

"Nate?" Here on the small space station in orbit, my strapped-down body was helpless.

"Nate?"

The part I didn't like about coming out of robot control was the waiting and wondering in the darkness and silence. I was totally dependent on Nate, the only other person on board the small space station.

"Nate?"

What if he didn't answer? What if something had happened to him? What if he'd somehow died? I'd be strapped in place with no way to move my hands. No way to remove the headset or blindfold. I'd be trapped until I, too, died.

"Nate?"

My heartbeat thudded in my ears. But that was the only sound I heard.

"Nate?"

Seconds later he pulled my headset off. Then my blind-fold.

"Sorry," he said as he began to unstrap me. "I was at the station's telescope. Took me a while to get here. I'm not that good at moving through weightlessness yet. You OK?"

"Could you leave the straps in place?" I asked. "I need to control a robot on Earth almost immediately."

"You have my full sympathy, bouncing around every-where."

"I just came back because I need to use the computer," I said. "Can you move to the computer and let me dictate to you an E-mail from your address? With no questions asked? I don't have time to explain."

"Sure." His big smile was reassuring.

He pushed himself away from the bed and toward the computer. When he reached it, he called over his shoulder, "Dictate away."

The computer had a permanent Internet connection via satellite. Without hesitation I called out my message. Nate began typing. When he was finished, he printed out a copy and brought it to me.

I scanned it to make sure it said everything I wanted. Dictating was more difficult than seeing the words on a screen.

From: "Nathan Guthrie" <guthrien@worldwidenet.com>
To: "Rawling McTigre" <mctigrer@marsdome.ss>
Sent: 04.07.2040, 09:28 P.M.
Subject: Where?

Rawling! Ignore the sender address at the top. It's me. Tyce. Remember, hard head against axle? No time to

*explain much. I know about you and Dad. Please estab-
lish your identity on a return E-mail by telling me where
you hung out with him in the downtime during your training sessions in New York. Much to tell later.*

Your friend, Tyce

It was close enough. The "hard head" phrase would be
enough for Rawling to know it actually was me. Once, on a
mission on Mars, I had bumped the robot's head against
the underside of a platform buggy and made a dumb joke
about it.

I didn't really need for Rawling to establish his identity
on his return E-mail. But I desperately needed to know
where they had hung out. By making it seem like I was
merely doing an identity check, it might throw off anyone
who might intercept the E-mail. I couldn't risk someone
else finding out that was my next destination in the robot
body I'd left behind with Ms. Borris.

"Looks good," I told Nate. "Can you fire it to Mars?"

He nodded and returned to the computer. "Sent," he
announced after hitting the keypad. "As promised, with no
questions asked."

"Thanks," I answered softly. Mars was so far away that
even at the speed of light, it would take a while for the message to cross the solar system and arrive at Rawling's computer at the Mars Dome. With luck, he'd be at his computer
and could reply immediately.

In the meantime, however, I couldn't rest.

Nate had set up a meeting with me and Cannon.

Back on Earth.

CHAPTER 21

"No, Tyce," Cannon said to my robot, "we can't simply take over a space station."

I was controlling a robot at the military base in D.C., and we sat in Cannon's small office.

"Dozens of countries each have their own in orbit," he continued. "According to international law, a space station is an extension of that country's territory. Attacking a space station, then, is an act of war. That's why you're so safe in the small one with Nate."

"But that remaining pod is orbiting somewhere around the Moon and it's got to be the one that belongs to the Manchurians. I talked to the kids through their robots. You're right. They're being held as slaves and forced to use their robots to work in the tantalum mine."

Cannon closed his eyes briefly. He rubbed his face. "My son is probably on that space station, then. Don't you think I want to begin a military operation to rescue him?"

"Then do it. Please."

"First," he said, "it would start an international incident that may lead to a third world war. At the very least it would destroy the Federation of countries that to date have somehow managed to work together in world peace and toward the colonization of Mars."

He sighed. "Second, even if I wanted to, there are still higher-ups in the military who would stop me. And third, even if I had permission, it would be an unsuccessful raid. The Manchurian space station's crew would have plenty of notice of our approach. All they would have to do is dump the kids into space. They would die instantly, float away, and we would never recover their bodies. We'd end up boarding an empty space station, and it would be a political disaster."

"But if you knew we could do nothing, why send me in a robot to confirm the robot-control slavery?" I wondered if my robot's voice reflected the stress I felt in my own body. It had been a long day, and it was now well past midnight.

"I was hoping," he said, "that the kids were somewhere on the Moon. Then it would have been far easier for a combat unit to approach quickly and unseen. And far more difficult for the Manchurians to move the kids or even hide their bodies."

"What you're telling me," I said through my robot, "is even though we know where they are . . . even though there's a real possibility that Dr. Jordan and Luke Daab are there too . . . still, we can't rescue the kids or capture Jordan or Daab?"

Thinking about Jordan and Daab made me shudder. After all, Dr. Jordan had tried to kill me before, and he'd tried to force Ashley to run a mission that would kill millions of people. The guy had no conscience. And Luke Daab— well, all he had done was rig our ship so that it would collide with the sun instead of arriving on Earth.

The general slowly nodded. "That's what I'm telling you. Unless you can think of something I can't." He stood. "And in the meantime, we have to do something about the other

216 kids now held hostage in Arizona. By our own Combat Force."

On my end, I took a deep breath. "Well, sir," I said, "I do have an idea about that. Would you be able to get some men loyal to you ready and waiting just outside the compound there?"

"Sure. We can have them there in an hour. Then what?"

"Hope and pray. In the meantime, I have a lot of robot control ahead of me."

I was about to disengage when someone knocked on the door.

"Sir?" The voice came from a man in uniform. I switched to a rear video lens and glanced at him. "Sir, I—"

"Not now!" Cannon barked at him.

It was too late for Cannon. The man in uniform had not guessed that I was currently controlling the robot. So I got a full look at the man's face.

It was the pilot! The man who had jumped out of the helicopter to leave us to crash! He was here? Working with Cannon?

"Tyce," Cannon said to my robot, "I can explain. Really."

I pretended I had already disengaged. If Cannon had double-crossed me, I didn't want him to know that I knew.

I woke up back on the space station. It was about 1:00 in the morning. And I was sick with worry.

Was Cannon on the Terrataker side? Would he have the Combat Force ready to help in Arizona? Or would he betray me?

"Nate," I called out, "anything back from Rawling on Mars?"

"Yup." Nate read me the E-mail.

"Next destination then, Nate." I grinned upward from

under my blindfold. I had to pretend everything was fine. I also desperately wanted to sleep. But there was no time. "Keep me moving. Back to the robot in New York."

My robot rolled off the street into a crowded coffee shop. It seemed that many of the people sitting at the tables wore shabby brown clothes and held their cups of coffee in both hands as if afraid someone might try to take them away. Cigarette smoke hung in the air like swirling fog.

Upon my appearance the low murmurs of conversation instantly turned into silence.

I knew they were all gawking at my robot. Unless they'd watched a lot of television over the last few days, they wouldn't know about robot control. Even so, the reaction wasn't so unusual. After all, what would you think if a nearly six-foot robot rolled into a place where you were having coffee?

"Greetings!" I said. "Is this a good place to get a cup of warm engine oil?"

People stood nervously and edged away from me. Some fled the coffee shop.

One man in a ragged brown suit shuffled toward me. His shoes were almost worn out, and his face was hidden by a threadbare baseball cap.

He got very close and whispered to my audio input speaker, "Engine oil? Couldn't you think of anything better than that?"

"Dad!" I whispered back. "It's good to see you!"

We sat in the backseat of a taxi. Dad had pulled his hat away from his face.

My robot body was bent at the waist to fit in, with my wheels above my midsection. It was like I'd been folded in half.

The taxi driver had just grunted when we got in the car. Evidently seeing a weird-looking robot and a homeless man together didn't even startle him.

Dad grinned. "Taxi drivers in New York have seen everything at least twice." Then he turned serious. "I doubt we have much time. I'm sure your robot has been reported by someone who saw it roll from the television studio to the coffee shop. From there the authorities will start pursuit."

I'd already explained to Dad how I got the name of the coffee shop from Rawling by return E-mail. Dad had promised to tell me everything else. Later. But first he had hustled us into a cab.

"Where are we going?" I asked.

"A computer expert," he said. "Ms. Borris and I spent a lot of time thinking this through. I think we have a chance. But you're going to have to learn fast."

"You're right," I said. "In about half an hour, I'm expected in Arizona."

I caught Dad's strange look out of the robot's side video lens.

"Long story," I said. "But I have to ask. Can we trust Cannon?"

"With our lives, Son."

If that was true, what about the pilot? But if there was anyone I would believe, it was Dad.

"Why do you ask?"

I answered. "I'll tell you more later. This is so complicated I hardly know where I am anymore. But if Ashley was able to get the ant-bot onto a soldier's sleeve like I asked just before getting into this robot, we might have a chance."

CHAPTER 22

"Mister," I said 40 minutes later, speaking softly through the ant-bot, "you have a lot of earwax."

I didn't know how Ashley had managed to get close enough to the soldier to put the ant-bot on his sleeve. All I knew was that she had done it. It had taken me 10 minutes to crawl up his sleeve. During that time, I'd heard three or four other soldiers address him as "Sergeant." So he was the one in control here. Ashley had picked the right person.

"Huh?" he said. "Who is that?"

"Does it matter? I'm inside your head." The sergeant did have a lot of earwax. I was very glad my ant-bot couldn't taste or smell. I had burrowed deep into his ear, deeper than any finger or Q-Tip could reach. And I intended to stay.

"Who is it?" he repeated, with panic in his voice. For the first time, even though I didn't quite know where this conversation was headed, I thought this crazy plan might work.

"Here's the truth," I spoke into the darkness of the bottom of his ear. "I am someone who can make your life miserable. Unless you listen to me."

"No!" The sergeant's panic grew. "It can't be you!"

I wondered who he thought I was. But I was willing to play along.

"Why can't it be me?" I asked.

He moaned. "I swear I had no choice. I thought enemy soldiers were about to take us. I thought you'd run away with me. When I found out you hadn't, it was too late to return to help."

"Chicken," I said.

"Please," he pleaded. "I've already been tortured by memories of you begging for me to come back. I didn't mean to leave you in battle. You don't need to haunt me more."

This guy believed in ghosts?

"Just unlock the rooms that hold the kids," I said. "Let them outside in the open area. Then I promise to leave you alone."

"No!"

"Oooooooh!" I raised the ant-bot's voice and tried the corny spooky ghost voice that you sometimes hear in really cheesy horror movies. *"Oooooooh! Leaving me alooooooone. Oooooooooh!"*

"Please! Please leave me!"

I notched up the volume. *"Oooooooooh! Oooooooooooh!"*

"Ouch!" he cried.

"I think," I said, "I'll sing you some of my favorite songs. I know about 100 of them."

I felt his head move. The darkness of the ear got even darker, as if he had clutched his head with both hands.

"Old MacDonald had a farm," I began in my best out-of-key voice, remembering when Mom used to tell me about Earth tunes and other things on Mars. I still hadn't seen a farm or a pig or a duck, but I sure knew how to sing about them. *"Ey-iy-ey-iy-oooooh! And on this farm he had a pig. Ey-iy-ey-iy-oooooh!"*

It was fun, singing, and I hit it with gusto. "With an *oink-oink* here. And an *oink-oink* there . . ."

"No! Normie, don't do this to me! I'm sorry I let you die!"

"Ducks next," I promised. It was really sad that he'd abandoned a friend. Sadder that he had all this guilt. But the lives of more than 200 kids were at stake. I was going to push hard. "Do you like ducks? *Quack? Quack?* I'm going to be spending a lot of time in your head. Day and night. Unless, of course, you let the kids outside."

"I can't! I can't!"

"Mooo! Mooo!"

"Please don't do this to me," he just continued to moan.

So I decided to try a different strategy. I reached out with one tiny ant-bot arm. Although I couldn't see what I was doing, I pinched as hard as I could.

"Ouch!"

I pinched and pinched. And *quacked* and *quacked*. And pinched and *mooed*. And pinched and *oinked*.

"Stop!"

I stopped.

"Just five minutes," he said. "If I let them out for five minutes, will you leave me alone?"

CHAPTER 23

"Here's the problem," I said to Nate back at the small space station when I had disengaged from the ant-bot. By now it was almost 2:00 A.M. on the morning of 04.07.2040. "Sound doesn't travel on the Moon. So I can't interview the robots in the tantalum mine."

It was a relief to be away from robot control, at least for a while. I was glad to be floating in the zero gravity of the space station. On Earth, 125,000 miles below, if one plan had gone right, Ashley and all the other kids were now outside the Parker, Arizona, mountain fortress and about to be rescued by Cannon's commando unit. If another plan went right, Dad and the computer expert guy in New York had used an access code given to Dad by Ms. Borris to get into a worldwide satellite feed that would also connect to the computer on Nate's and my space station. On this end, all I had to do was enter the access code they had given me.

"Interview?" Nate had not shaved since we'd left Earth by shuttle. He rubbed the beginning of the dark bristles on his chin as he gave me a quizzical look.

"Cannon said there was no way to send in a military force." I grinned. "So let's send in the entire world."

I looked down at the space station's mainframe. It didn't take long to keyboard the right access code. But I was far from finished.

"Send in the entire world . . ."

The next part was tricky. It involved tinkering with connector cables and hardware. I knew I needed to concentrate, but I was so tired that it felt like I was wearing heavy rubber gloves. That's where robots have a distinct advantage. They never get tired. They go until they run out of battery power, then stop. Me, I needed sleep.

I rubbed my eyes and strained to look for the right plug-ins. I needed to connect the mainframe to the robot-control computer. No one had ever tried this before, but the computer expert thought it wouldn't be a problem. Of course, he wasn't on a space station, halfway between Earth and the Moon himself. Nor was he the person about to hook himself up to both computers.

"*Ey-iy-ey-iy-oooooh* . . . ," I hummed to myself. Anything to stay awake. Somehow the tune had stuck in my brain, and I was having a hard time getting it out. "With a *moo-moo* here. And a *moo-moo* there. *Ey-iy-ey-iy-oooooh* . . ."

"Tyce!" Nate's voice broke in.

"Huh?"

"You all right?"

"Yeah." I snapped a connection in place. If I had it wired right . . .

"Tyce. You didn't answer my question. Send in the entire world?"

I rubbed my face again. "Virtual reality," I said. "It's like the real thing."

"Pardon?" Nate asked. "You're slurring your words."

I slapped my face a few times. "Virtual reality. We send the world there. Or we send there to the world."

"Buddy, I'm worried about you."

"I'm worried about me too," I said. All I wanted to do was sleep. Five minutes. That's all I needed. Five more minutes of staying awake. "Can you help get me ready for robot control one last time?"

Back in the tantalum mine, I found the robot exactly where I had left it. In the shadows of a man-size hole gouged into a shaft dug by other robots.

I rolled forward.

All of the other robots were busy with their giant torches.

Except for a video monitor, they were not under supervision by any adults in space suits.

This made sense, of course. The kids themselves were held hostage on the Manchurian space station. They had no place to escape, no matter what the robots they controlled on the Moon below them might do. So why waste space-suit time for adults? Just give the kids their assignment and work them mercilessly. The whole thing made me feel sick.

When I reached another robot, I touched its arm with mine.

The robot stopped cutting into rock.

It watched as I bent over and scratched some words on the Moon dirt, glad that English had evolved into a standard language across the world. These kids had all been kidnapped from different countries and had all been robbed of the one place most important for anyone. Home. Something that maybe they'd finally find if we could get them released.

I finished scratching and let the kid who controlled the robot see what I had written. The robot clapped its hands together, movement that drew other robots closer.

Finally all of them crowded around to read the ground. And all started clapping. It had only taken four simple words.

Time to go home.

CHAPTER 24

Suits. I had never worn one on Mars. So this was a first. I decided I hated them. Especially stiff navy blue, with a white shirt underneath that itched. And a tie that cut off my air supply. I was glad it wasn't standard issue on Mars. But Ms. Borris had knotted the tie for me and told me to quit fussing. Dad had laughed the whole time I had tried pushing her away.

"Show time," Ms. Borris said, with an uncharacteristic grin on her face.

"Wonderful," I said. I made a face at Ashley. She knew what I meant. It was anything but.

Yesterday, two hours after my robot had made contact with the other robots at the tantalum mine, a space shuttle had taken Nate and me back to Earth. After a quick flight to New York, I was ready—finally—for a good night's sleep.

This morning, the most wonderful thing happened. I woke up to my dad's smiling face.

And now I was about to face the World United Federation ethics committee—again. But at least I knew what to expect from the Vice-Governors this time.

The door to the waiting room opened, and a Combat Force soldier nodded in my direction.

Dad knew better than to push my wheelchair for me. I hated it when anyone did that. It made me feel weak and helpless.

I gripped the arms and rolled forward. Alone. And nervous, yet somehow confident too.

The decision of the ethics committee would determine the future of robot control. Which would determine the direction of human history. I guess that was important enough to wear a suit. Even if it was uncomfortable and itchy.

I passed through the door and moved down the hallway.

The Combat Force soldier escorted me into a quiet chamber where all seven gray-haired men waited for me. The chamber where I had already faced them as I controlled a robot.

Now it was me.

In my wheelchair.

In my suit.

Show time.

None of the Vice-Governors spoke for the first five minutes.

Instead the lights were dimmed and video footage played on a large screen at the front of the chamber. I knew the footage. It had played for the entire world the day before, while I was still in the space station halfway between the Earth and the Moon.

It showed the interior of the Manchurian Sector space station that orbited the Moon. The kids were lined up in neat rows, suspended in giant jelly tubes. A voice-over played during this eerie scene.

"My name is Ingrid Sosktychek. I am 12 years old. When I was too young to remember, I was taken from my parents. I was trained in robot control on Earth. Two years ago I was moved here onto this space station. Twelve hours a day I control a robot that digs rock in a mine on the Moon. For the other 12 hours I am put to sleep and fed through tubes. Twice now my body has outgrown the tube that holds me. There are 24 of us on this space station. Please help."

The video footage showed as much as Ingrid could see through her own eyes as she turned her head within the tube that held her body. Then it went blank.

The blankness didn't surprise me. That happened when an adult monitoring the tantalum mine through surveillance cameras noticed two robots not moving. The worker rushed in wearing a space suit and disconnected the robots—mine and Ingrid's—from each other. By then, of course, it was too late.

Ingrid had spoken to the world.

Here in the chamber, the lights grew brighter again.

"Gentlemen," Vice-Governor Patterson began, "I cannot presume all of you saw this yesterday when it broke live into all the major network programming. Even if you did see it then, or in subsequent newscasts, I want to remind you of the horror and abuse that is capable with robot control."

"I'm still not sure how all of it was broadcast," Vice-Governor Armitage said. "The technology of this is far too confusing."

"We'll let Tyce Sanders answer."

They looked at me.

I swallowed. So far it didn't sound like they were going to vote in favor of robot control. But robot control wasn't the

129

problem. It was the humans who took advantage of the technology and decided to abuse powerless people, like the 24 kids who were forced to operate the robots on the Moon.

"I can't explain exactly how it works," I said, "because I can't explain everything about how computers work. What I can tell you, though, is that I was able to reverse the information flow. Usually the robots give and take information to the brain. This time a bypass allowed Ingrid to send what she saw and heard through her robot circuits into mine. That was relayed to my computer on board the U.S. space station, where I was, and patched into a satellite feed."

In the tantalum mine, I'd made the connection from Ingrid's robot to my robot and then had immediately disengaged so I no longer controlled my robot. That turned my robot into a simple computer, and it continued to send information to our space station computer. Because Ms. Borris, before her disappearance, had been able to supply Dad with the codes that accessed the worldwide television network mainframe, it had been easy to hack into the network and feed the images to the entire world.

"I think I understand the basic concept," Vice-Governor Michaels said after a few moments. His voice echoed in the quiet of the chamber. "And I would like to point out to my esteemed committee members that while this footage is an example of the horror possible with robot control, it is also an example of a problem solved by robot control."

Other Vice-Governors nodded. This was good. I hoped.

"Furthermore," Vice-Governor Michaels said, "I would like to draw your attention to the incident in Arizona."

Yes. Arizona. Where Cannon's commando group had been able to succeed in the relatively easy task of rescuing all the other kids outside the fortress.

"There," Vice-Governor Michaels continued, "we have another example of the decisions made by adults that impact these children. From what I understand, the sergeant there realized it was wrong to hold them captive and arranged to release them to a waiting rescue group."

Hah, I thought. The sergeant there just didn't want to let people know he thought he'd been haunted by a terrible singer and an old friend named Normie. But I would keep this secret.

"What are you saying?" Vice-Governor Armitage asked.

Vice-Governor Michaels answered. "Let's switch briefly to some more video I've asked to be made ready for this meeting."

The lights lowered. And there I was. Actually, there my robot was. Speaking to Ms. Borris in the interview.

"If there were 200 of you orbiting in space and all 200 of you controlled armed robots down here on Earth, wouldn't you be perfect soldiers? Don't you see potential danger in that?" she queried.

"Who would build the 200 armed robots? Who would put them in place?" I responded.

"I suppose it would be military people."

"Then maybe you should ask them those questions."

Immediately the lights brightened.

"It seems to me," Vice-Governor Michaels said, "that this young man makes an excellent point. And let's not overlook the fact that he made it through the voice of a robot. It is still a human mind behind the robot. As he and the others grow older, they will still make decisions with their human minds. The robots are simply tools, like any other tools."

He paused. "And yes, they can be weapons. Just as a simple kitchen knife can be used to cut bread or attack another person. My first point is this. There is nothing good or bad about the robots themselves. The issue we face is a much larger one. Controlling the intent of the people in power. And the events of the last few weeks, including the assassination attempt at the Summit of Governors, show that our children seem much more capable of doing what is right than some of those in power. More importantly, the power that the robots give them has allowed them to stop the very abuse the adults attempted."

Silence greeted that.

"My biggest concern," Vice-Governor Michaels said, "is the possible damage to the children. They had no choice when they were operated on. Yet the operation is not possible on humans old enough to make the choice. Which means we must make a clear choice. Impose a worldwide ban on robot control and stop this technology or—"

"That would only drive it underground," Vice-Governor Armitage protested. "Where only those with the power to abuse will have children who control robots. And I think we all know who I'm talking about."

Vice-Governor Michaels smiled. "Exactly. Or we continue with robot control openly and embrace all the good that can come of it, while yet protecting ourselves and these children against the misuse of their persons and the technology. We need not look any further than the nuclear-plant incident to see how much this can help mankind. And then, of course, there is the Mars Project."

"I protest!" Vice-Governor Calvin said sternly. "Look at the young man in front of you. He is in a wheelchair. This was inflicted upon him without his consenting to the risk."

Vice-Governor Michaels smiled again, calmly. "I agree. What I was going to propose is that every child who receives the operation is given the choice, when old enough, to continue with robot control or leave it. No child shall ever be forced to control robots."

"That is all very good," Vice-Governor Calvin persisted, "but it doesn't address those children who suffer damage during surgery. If Tyce never wanted to control a robot again, he cannot go back to a normal life."

"Excellent point," Vice-Governor Michaels countered. "I will address it two ways. First, his was the pioneer operation. Not only that, but it was done on Mars, without the proper equipment in case of an emergency. Since then, no other child has suffered damage. And second—" he paused and looked directly at me—"if damage is done to a child, all the resources available to us shall be used to help that individual child."

I wasn't sure I understood.

"What I propose is this," Vice-Governor Michaels said to the others. "We form a set of guidelines that allow robot control to be used ethically and fairly. And guidelines that protect the welfare of the children involved in it. How many vote yes?"

All hands went up. Some slowly. Some quickly. But all went up.

"My second proposal, then, is part of the first. No matter what the cost to us, we undo the harm that has been done to Tyce Sanders. And in the future to any other children."

My heart began to pound. Had I understood him correctly?

But it couldn't be. There was no way the harm done to me could be reversed.

I turned to look at my dad and was surprised to see tears in his eyes.

"Gentlemen," Vice-Governor Michaels said to the rest of the chamber, "I have consulted extensively with medical experts over the last day. They tell me a successful operation on Tyce Sanders is possible. It will be difficult and very expensive, but it's possible. If we vote to allocate funds, Tyce Sanders may someday soon be able to walk."

Walk?

This time, all hands went up instantly.

Walk?

I finally understood.

Walk!

EPILOGUE

04.08.2040

It took five hours after the ethics committee meeting for everything to settle down. I got tired of smiling for all the reporters afterward. To my surprise, all the Vice-Governors voted "Yes" to continuing robot control—as long as guidelines could be set to keep children from being abused, as they'd been in Arizona, in the Manchurian Sector space station, and in the eight other pods of robot kids we'd discovered around the world.

I'm finally back in Dad's and my room at the Combat Force base outside New York City. I'm exhausted and yet, somehow, I can't sleep. Questions and answers keep running through my mind and mixing with each other.

As soon as Ingrid's live interview flashed across the world, Ms. Borris was released by the high-ranking military people. The barrage of information released to the world had uncloaked so much that they didn't dare press charges against her for breaking national security laws. She met Nate and me as soon as we stepped off our flight to New York. . . .

I was interrupted by a knock on the door. Dad had left a half hour ago to talk with Ms. Borris and the general. "Come on in." I had nothing to be afraid of now. Like there was any reason to lock your door at a military base anyway.

Ashley stepped in and quietly closed the door. She slumped into the chair next to me and kicked off her shoes. "Wow, am I tired," she said.

That was the understatement of the world.

"Yeah, me too."

"You know," she said softly, "it was nice—for at least a few hours—to be part of a real family . . . even if it seemed like it was difficult to fit in with those two who claimed to be my parents."

I nodded. It had taken a long time for me to feel like I knew my dad and that he was part of our family. Especially since he had spent so much time over the years away from us as a space pilot and . . .

My head still spun over Ms. Borris's words—that Dad was actually an agent for the U.S. military, fighting against the Terratakers. Boy, did we have a lot to talk about when he got back to the room. Some of the little things that had happened since we landed on Earth were now starting to make sense. It had all been a setup, to protect Dad from being revealed as an agent within the U.S. division of the Combat Force.

I had so many questions. I yawned. If I could stay awake until he got back to the room, that is. . . .

"Tyce," Ashley jumped in, "are you really going to do it? Think about having the operation where you could walk again?"

I was quiet for a couple of minutes.

Finally I said the only thing I could. "I don't know. If it means I might lose the ability to control robots . . ."

"It's OK if you don't want to talk about it now," Ashley said quickly, with her eyes on the floor. "But I just wanted you to know that whatever you decide is OK with me. . . ."

With those few words she got up, picked up her shoes, and dangled them in her hands as she walked toward the door.

"And Tyce?" she said just before she stepped into the hallway. "You're the closest person to family I'll ever have."

Then, with the glitter of a tear in her eye and a flash of her silver cross earring, Ashley was gone.

I sat motionless, thinking and fingering the other silver cross she'd given me as a gift a long time ago, when she thought we might have to say good-bye for a long time. Then, slowly, my hands moved back to the keyboard.

Sometimes life just seems so unfair. Like how people can abuse kids by sticking them in jelly tubes and making them control robots without having a life. But even with things like that happening in the world, I've come to believe that God is still in control. People can use things for evil, but, as Mom says, "God always intends things for good."

And she's right. There is no doubt now that the kids on the space station orbiting the Moon are going to be released. With all the public, worldwide pressure, the Manchurians have already released a press statement that the children will be released

as soon as transportation will allow it. Further,
they claim to be horrified that one of their space
stations was being used for such a purpose as
child slavery. That is their claim. But one by one,
other countries that once backed the Manchurians
have begun to distance themselves publicly from
them.

In an effort to sway public opinion, the Manchurians have promised to launch a search, via the
children's DNA and all known hospital DNA
records. They're also asking parents of missing
children to supply blood samples for DNA testing,
all in an effort to find the children's parents, match-
ing the search that the Americans are doing for the
kids in Arizona. The Manchurian promises might
not be enough. On Earth, at least, the Manchurians
look like they are on a downward slide.

As for linking all the children with their parents,
it will take a while. I'm just glad it worked out in
Arizona as planned. But I would like to know why
the general and the helicopter pilot . . .

I stopped keyboarding and let other questions flood into
my mind. . . . What about Dr. Jordan and Luke Daab? They
hadn't yet been located. Had they given up fighting for the
Terratakers?

And the question that meant the most for the Earth's
future: Would the theory of the carbon-dioxide generators
speed along an atmosphere for Mars? Could it become
inhabitable for humans outside the dome?

I sighed. All of these questions certainly weren't helping
put me to sleep.

Just then the door opened again. It was Dad, looking

exhausted but happy. His tie hung crookedly against his shirt, which was open at the neck. I'd long ago shed my ethics committee attire for a comfortable Combat Force jumpsuit I'd found in the closet of our room.

"Information on the Moon pod was just released to the public," Dad said. "And Chad, the general's son, is supposedly among the kids who will soon be shuttled to Earth. We're still waiting to see if the Supreme Governor's grandson comes up on the list too. He was kidnapped about the same time as Chad."

"Did you have a chance to ask Cannon about the helicopter pilot?"

Dad nodded. "We can talk more about that later," he said. "But, Tyce, remember the kind of pressure that was being put on Cannon. His own son was a hostage in the pod."

"Big pressure," I agreed.

"And remember that all of this has hinged on world public opinion. Cannon knew if the media finally exposed all of this, his son would be safe. But Cannon couldn't betray the military faction that wanted all of this kept secret."

"With you so far. But that doesn't explain the helicopter pilot who tried to kill us, then shows up later in his office."

"The pilot didn't try to kill you. At Cannon's instructions, he made it look that way. Cannon was ready to take over the controls."

I didn't get it. "Cannon wanted it that way?"

"Remember the bomb in your wheelchair and that last-minute rescue? Ever wonder how they knew about the bomb? Cannon put it there. He set the whole thing up. He had to."

"Because . . ."

"It began to shift public opinion. He knew the hidden

Terratakers in the Combat Force would have no choice but to do everything possible to protect you. In short, he disarmed them, knowing they would have liked you out of the way."

I let out a deep breath. "But he couldn't ever tell me in case the listening devices were nearby."

"Exactly." Dad walked over to me and put a hand on my shoulder. "Tyce, I'm really proud of you. For going ahead with the mission to help the kids, even without me. For everything you're doing with the robots. For appearing before the ethics committee . . ."

He tousled my hair. Less than a year ago, when I didn't like him very much, I would have hated that. Now I didn't mind.

"Thanks, Dad," I said. Then I grinned. "Don't you think it's about time to do what I told the robots in the tantalum mine? 'Time to go home'?"

"You bet," he said enthusiastically.

It *was* time. Time for us to go back to our *real* home. A place with a butterscotch sky and blue sun.

Mars.

And I couldn't wait. . . .

IS DNA JUST ABOUT FINGERPRINTS?

Did you know that your body comes with a complete set of instructions?

This "master blueprint," called a *genome,* is what told your mother's body to make you into a human being instead of a frog or a dog or a cat. It's what makes you *you,* instead of your brother or sister. And you're still carrying that genome even as you grow up. It will never change.

A genome consists of *DNA* (you can think of DNA as the "building blocks of life") and associated protein molecules contained in something called *chromosomes.* The nucleus of each human cell contains two sets of chromosomes. One's from your dad. The other is from your mom.

The way it all works together is pretty complicated but also very cool. And scientists today are still trying to figure out how our bodies work. That's why the United States started the Human Genome Project in 1990—to figure out how to identify people's genes and map DNA. Currently it's being used to test babies for any genetic problems before they're born and to screen newborn babies. Mapping someone's DNA can even tell if someone is high-risk to develop cancer or confirm the diagnosis of a genetic disease. It can tell you how long you'll probably live. And it can even ID a criminal!

All of these are very good things, but there's also the risk of taking them too far. In Tyce's world of 2040, the Terratakers are arguing that everyone should be automatically tested, without having a say in it. And that means the DNA test results will have to be stored somewhere. That also means that those test results can fall into the wrong people's hands—people like Dr. Jordan, Luke Daab, and other Terratakers who want to identify skills, like those of the robot kids, that they can abuse.

It also means that suddenly those with "perfect" genes will become the highly prized people. Those with "imperfect" DNA—who have genetic defects or even those who aren't as "smart" as others—can become less important to the world. They can be considered "not fully human"—like the Vice-Governor who seemed to imply that Tyce isn't as good as other humans because he's in a wheelchair. And that kind of thinking can lead to some scary things down the road. Like what happened to the Jews in concentration camps in the days of World War II and Hitler. They were considered a "non-human" race just because they were Jews.

So although these leaps ahead in science, like the Human Genome Project, can be good and can identify what's "unique" about you through your individual human genome, they can't and don't tell you what God does. He's the one who has made you with your particular, individual genes. That means in his eyes you're perfect—just as you are. No matter if your nose or teeth are crooked, you can't throw a baseball, or you can't run as fast as your sister. It also means that he has something special in mind for your life.

Just look at Tyce. Even though he's in a wheelchair, he was able to save the lives of millions of people at the Los Angeles nuclear plant. And, because of his special skills, he figured out a unique way to rescue the robot kids near the Moon.

It all comes down to this. Your DNA and chromosomes—what makes your physical body—aren't what's most important. Instead, what makes you really human is that you've been created by God, implanted with a soul, and that only you, as a human, can have a relationship with God.

Your DNA isn't just about your fingerprints or your skills. It's actually God's fingerprint on you.

ABOUT THE AUTHOR

Sigmund Brouwer, his wife, recording artist Cindy Morgan, and their daughter split living between Red Deer, Alberta, Canada, and Nashville, Tennessee. He has written several series of juvenile fiction and eight novels. Sigmund loves sports and plays golf and hockey. He also enjoys visiting schools to talk about books. He welcomes visitors to his Web site at www.coolreading.com, where he and a bunch of other authors like to hang out in cyberspace.

MARS

DIARIES

are you ready?

Set in an experimental community on Mars, the Mars Diaries feature 14-year-old Tyce Sanders. Life on the red planet is not always easy, but it is definitely exciting. As Tyce explores his strange surroundings, he also finds that the mysteries of the planet point to his greatest discovery— a new relationship with God.

MISSION 1: OXYGEN LEVEL ZERO
Can Tyce stop the oxygen leak in time?

MISSION 2: ALIEN PURSUIT
What attacked the tekkie in the lab?

MISSION 3: TIME BOMB
What mystery is uncovered by the quake?

MISSION 4: HAMMERHEAD
Will the comet crash on Earth, destroying all life?

MISSION 5: SOLE SURVIVOR
Will a hostile takeover destroy the Mars Project?

MISSION 6: MOON RACER
Who's really controlling the spaceship?

MISSION 7: COUNTDOWN
Will there be enough time to save the others?

MISSION 8: ROBOT WAR
Will the rebels succeed with their plan?

MISSION 9: MANCHURIAN SECTOR
Can Tyce find—and save—the others like him?

News Bulletin from Tyce...
New Missions are now in stores!!

mars DIARIES

Mission Registration	Red Planet	Tyce's Journal	Rawling's Quiz	Mars and Beyond	Meet the Author

OOK DATA • • ● ① ② ③ ④ ⑤ ⑥ ⑦ ⑧

LOG IN:

YOU ARE
HERE

MARS

cy Policy

Visit Tyce on-line!

- ○ Learn more about the red planet from a
  real expert
- ○ Great contests and awesome prizes
- ○ Fun quizzes and games
- ○ Find out when the next book is coming out

mars DIARIES

Discover the latest news about the Mars Diaries.
Visit www.marsdiaries.com

SIGMUND BROUWER'S

COOLWRITING SOFTWARE

EXPERT HELP FOR STUDENT WRITERS

Make your computer an awesome writing tool! **coolwriting** software gives you instant help for your stories, poems, and essays. Like a trusted friend with the answers you need, **coolwriting** is there to help with your writing—while you're typing on your computer. You're sure to improve in skill and confidence with **coolwriting**. Why not test it out? There's a free demo on the **coolwriting** Web site:

http://www.coolreading.com/coolwriting

COME INTO THE COOL